THIS & THAT

GENEALOGY - HISTORY
OVERTON COUNTY TN

VOLUME 1

BY RONALD DISHMAN

VERBA VOLENT, SCRIPTA MANET
Celerus Books

ISBN: 978-1-60414-115-3

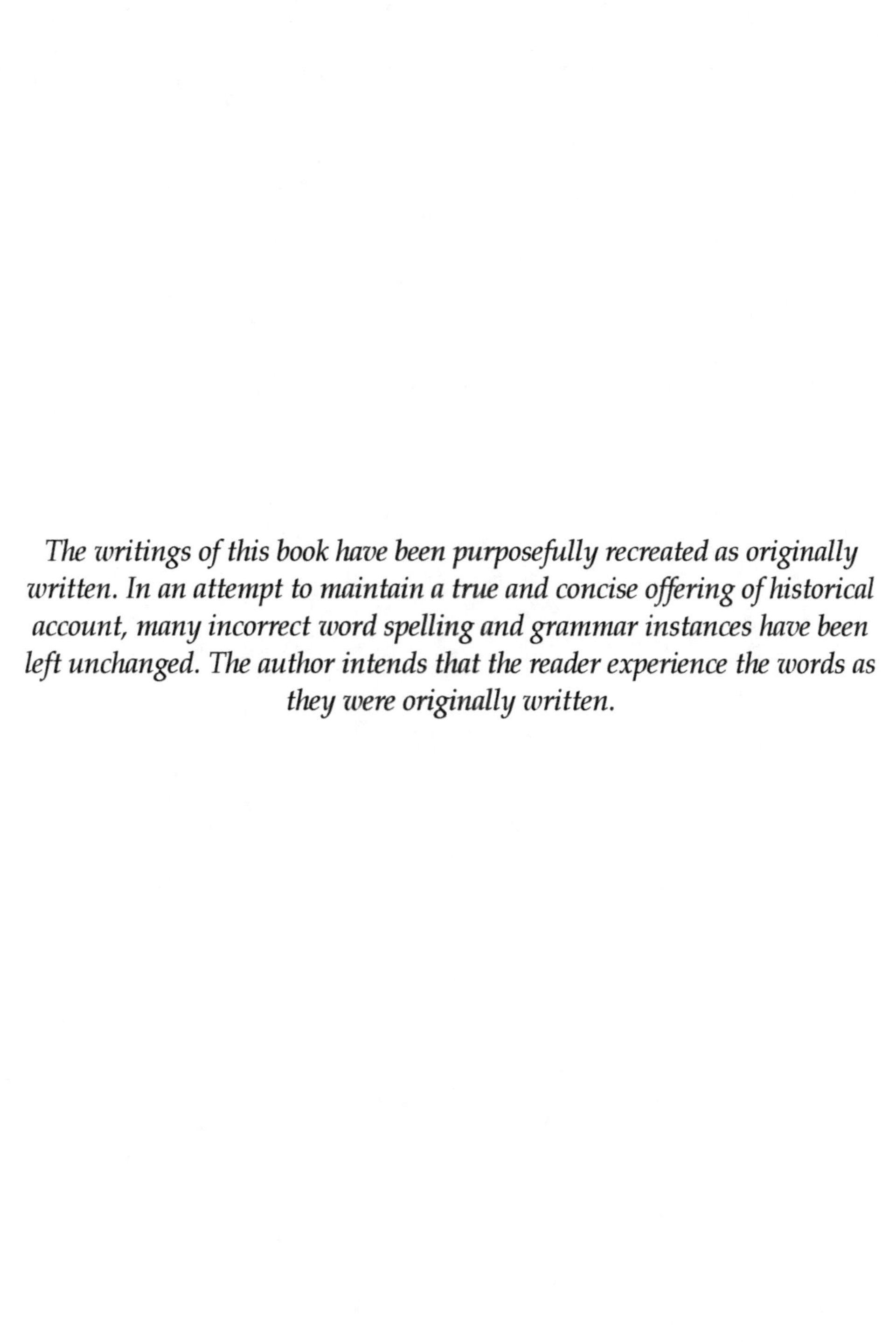

The writings of this book have been purposefully recreated as originally written. In an attempt to maintain a true and concise offering of historical account, many incorrect word spelling and grammar instances have been left unchanged. The author intends that the reader experience the words as they were originally written.

CONTENTS

SECTION I
Genealogy

SECTION II
General History

SECTION III
Military

Introduction

This book is a combination of exactly what the title states—this and that genealogy and history, along with photographs taken from various sources, including newspapers, court records, and other sources that may be included with individual articles.

These documents have been collected over a 30 year period and painstakingly recorded into what has become this book. I hope others can enjoy them as I have. This is volume one. I hope that many follow…

Sincerely,

Ronald Dishman

P.O. Box 283

Livingston TN 38570

931 823 1156

Email: researcher@twlakes.net

SECTION I
GENEALOGY

ALBERT ARMSTRONG, DESCENDANT
EARLY PIONEERS, SUCCUMBS
Services Held at Bethlehem Church Tuesday For Aged
Overton County Native of Livingston
By: R. L. Mitchell Jr.

Albert M. Armstrong 75 died Monday having been stricken with a nervous breakdown some two years ago from which he recuperated to a limited extent but never fully recovered. His condition had grown more serious for the past few months and for the past few days those familiar with his condition realized that his end was near.

He was endowed with a strong constitution and was equally strong mentally. Both paternal and maternal grandparents came from sturdy pioneer families from Kentucky and North Carolina and settled at Monroe more than 125 years ago, his paternal grandfather being Landon Armstrong who figured prominently in the creation of Overton county and to its subsequent organization and died after the Civil War.

Among the brothers of hid grandfather was Judge Thomas M. Armstrong, whose sons Capt. Tim Armstrong and Capt. Tom Armstrong respectively, operated steamboats on the Cumberland River for several years.

His maternal grandfather was the late Judge Alvin Cullom who was a statesman and jurist of renowned figuring largely in the affairs of Overton county before the Civil War and in the affairs of the state and nation as well. He too survived the Civil War but being a Southerner lost heavily in that three sons were killed and h is property was consumed and destroyed.

Pleasant M. Armstrong father of the subject of this article was during his early manhood and prior to the War Between the States a successful merchant and business man and was prominent in the business and political affairs of this county and section. When the unfortunate break came between the North and the South in 1861 he cast his fortune with the South he loved so well. His sons Cull and Cross being of military age volunteered in 1861 for service in the Confederate army, the eldest Cull, serving as lieutenant. Both were killed. Besides the loss of his sons on account of their courage and daring his slaves were freed and his property carried away or destroyed by the Federal soldiers so that he was repressed beyond recovery passing away in sorrow some time after Robert E. Lee's surrender.

Albert M. Armstrong was born in Livingston and spent his entire life in and near Livingston. He was generous to a fault possessing many admirable traits of character, had many friends and for some time he was a successful hardware salesman, representing the old reliable firm of A. M. Tenison & Son of Nashville. He was also a skilled painter by trade, following his profession for many years. Some time after he had been overtaken by affliction so that he could not work, he became more interested in the Bible and read it as a student and about one year ago he was converted to the Christian religion and at his request was baptized by Elder Kerby Smith.

Surviving are two sisters Mrs. Lula A. Deep widow of the late Jas. P. Deep of Glasgow, KY, and Miss Belle Armstrong, also of Glasgow, besides many nieces and nephews and other relatives.

Funeral services were conducted Tuesday at Bethlehem Church by the Rev. A. A. D. Smith, of the Presbyterian Church, with burial at the Bethlehem cemetery.

THE CULLOM FAMILY
By: Albert R. Hogue
Jamestown, Tenn.
June 20, 1952

Born June 4, 1810 in Elk Spring Valley near Monticello KY, Gen. William Cullom died in Clinton Tenn. in 189-.

His father was William Cullom a farmer his mother Elizabeth Northcraft. They came from Wayne county KY and settled in Overton county where his two sons, Alvin and Edward N. and two daughters

Mrs. Elizabeth McHenry and Mrs. Lucinda Hart were living at the time.

Elizabeth married Dr. Spencer McHenry of Overton county. Lucinda married John Hart Sr. who served as County Court Clerk in the 80's.

Other brothers and sisters were: Tilman, who fought under Gen. William Henry Harrison in the War of 1812; Edward N. who moved to Illinois and served several times in the state legislature of that state. He was a member of the convention that framed the first constitution of that state.

Richard N. also moved to Illinois and became the father of Shelly M. Cullom who served as a speaker in the Illinois legislature governor of Illinois and for many years a U. S. Senator.

Alvin Cullom lived in Overton county and died there. He served two terms in Congress and was noted lawyer.

James N. married a sister of A. W. O. Totten who served on the Supreme Court bench of Tennessee Circuit Judges B. C. and James Totten, The Tottens lived originally in Monroe in Overton county at the time. Adam Huntsman afterwards congressman and John Catron who later became a Judge in the Supreme Court of the United States lived there.

Susan Cullom married Alfred Phillips. She like her brothers Edward N. and Tilman moved to Illinois and died there.

Permelia Cullom married William Brown a Methodist minister.

Gen. William Cullom was admitted to the bar and began the practice of law at Gainesboro. In 1835 he was elected Attorney General of his district and served six years. He afterwards was elected to the State Senate in 1851 he was elected to Congress and served two terms. While a member of Congress he distinguished himself but his out spoken opposition to the Kansas-Nebraska bill. He was a close personal friend of Henry Clay and he and Governor James C. Jones were present when Henry Clay died.

Governor John C. Brown appointed Cullom Attorney-General of the 16th Judicial District in 1872. He held this office for 12 years. His home at the time was at Clinton in Roane County. Court records in Overton and Fentress show that he had a large practice in these and adjoining counties.

The Cullom family and related families have been leaders in the agricultural, ethical and educational fields in this section during its history.

Among the more recent distinguished members of the family was the late Chancellor Charles J. Cullom Jr. who is a lawyer at the Livingston bar, but now in the armed services. Mrs. Mary Cullom widow of Charles J. Cullom is the present Clerk and Master of Overton County.

April 27, 1934
Early Obituaries told much family history like the one
of J.C. Thomas age 90 that appeared in the local paper.

DEATH COMES TO J. C. THOMAS 90 AFTER LONG SIEGE
Prominent Overton Resident Dies at Home of son Friday
Burial at Flatt Creek

James C. Thomas 90 the oldest in the western part of Overton County and with one exception the oldest in the entire county and perhaps the best and most favorably known citizen in this section died Friday at the home of his youngest son James Harris Thomas with whom he had lived the most of the time since the death of his wife twenty two years ago. His death came after a lingering illness of several months. He came from two pioneer families his father Byrd Thomas being a native of Bledsoe County where he was elected and served as High Sheriff from 1848 to 1852 when he died in 1852. James C. Thomas was born in Bledsoe county June 10, 1844 his mothers maiden name was Deborah Masters and came of a pioneer family of Overton county. She was a sister to Isaac G. Masters of the Flatt Creek community who passed away a few years ago at the ripe old age of 94 years. She was a first cousin to the late Col. William Gore who fought in the Mexican War as Colonel and also served in the Confederate army 1861 to 1865 and Col. Mounce Gore who was a gallant Colonel in the Confederate army and who is the father of our Federal Judge the Honorable John J. Gore whose home is at Gainesboro. Another cousin of Mrs. Debora Thomas was the late Elvira Poteet who was postmaster at Netherland for many years. She was also related to the Goodbar family who were prominent in this county from 1835 to 1865. In 1854 soon after the death of his father James C. Thomas with his mother and three sisters and two brothers came to this county with his mother's relatives and he spent the remainder of his life here. He was married in 1866 to Miss Mary Ann Harris daughter of the late O.H.P. Harris who was Circuit Court Clerk of this county for many years and was one of its outstanding citizens. He was an energetic farmer and manifested much interest in church and educational affairs serving as school director several years. He had been an active of the Church of Christ for more than sixty years. He led and exemplary life and will be missed in the home church and the community where he lived. Surviving are his children as follows Joseph Byrd Thomas, James Harris Thomas, both of Overton county, Mrs. Amelia Wells of Watertown and Mrs. Harvey G. Gragg of Algood, and by seven grandchildren, and fourteen grandchildren, Besides his own children he reared and educated three nephews, sons of his deceased sister who were orphans one of whom is at this time a prominent minister in the church of Christ. Funeral services were conducted at the home of his eldest son J. Byrd Thomas neat the Flatt Creek cemetery by Dr. Thomas A. Langford of the Church of Christ Friday afternoon in the presence of a large crowd. Burial was at the Flatt Creek cemetery.

August 30, 1935 Article

JAMES A. DAUGHERTY VISITS HIS OLD HOME

James A. Daugherty and his wife of Nashville came to Livingston Sunday September 1st for the purpose of spending a few days with his sister Mrs. Sibba D. Chapin who is living at the Brown Hotel in Livingston Mrs. Chapin has been quite ill and confined in the Cookeville hospital for several weeks until recently. Her condition is decidedly better. James A. Daugherty was born and reared in Livingston but has made his home in Nashville for the past forty years. He is now in the grain brokerage business.

E. W. SEWELL VISITS OLD HOME

Mr. E. W. Eldon Sewell of Pawnee, Okla., while on his way to visit his old home in Pickett county visited with friends in Livingston last Friday and Saturday. Mr. Sewell is in his 81st year and is very active for his age. He drives his own car wherever he goes and has traveled over a large portion of the United States during the last few years. Mr. Sewell was born in Pickett County near Byrdstown but at that time was Overton county. He sat on the first jury, the first court ever held in Byrdstown. The court was held in the upper story of the building now occupied by J. H. Robbins & Son. Mr. Sewell went to Texas in 1883. He made his first trip back here two years after being away 52 years. He has worked 19 years among the Indian tribes of the west for the government. In 1905 was appointed instructor for cement work wagon making and blacksmithing in the government school for Indians at Ft. Mojova, Arizona transferred in 1917 to the school at Albuquerque, New Mexico where he remained until retiring from the service in 1924. Mr. Sewell has a very interesting collection of handiwork made by the Navajo Indians which include blankets had worked silver and bead work.

Overton County Deed book Y page 461-462

Deed specifies request of Mary Copeland to be buried beside her late husband J. S. Copeland at her death she reserves life estate dated 1885 December 8th. I have included the original copy below because of the beautiful handwriting and that is was legible enough to read.

Mary Copeland

Deed

J. C. Hall

Whereas by the Statutes of Will I Mary Copeland am lawfully seized of a life estate in a tract of land in the State of Tennessee, Overton County and district No. 6. Containing by estimation 150 acres more or less, and bounded as follows:

Beginning at a stake in the lane between me and Col. John W. Hall; running with a road up the mountain to the Burksville road, and with said road to the top of the Mountain: thence to C. H. P. Harris' now John Hart's line Corner; thence with Thos Wray's line to the Mouth of a lane leading to my House: thence with the lane and road to the beginning. Now for the Consideration of $20.00 Dollars a year to be paid on the first of the year, I have bargained and sold and do hereby Convey my said life estate in the said tract of land to one J. C. Hall to have and to hold to the said J. C. Hall for and during the term of my natural life, the title to which for the said term I do warrant and agree to defend against the lawful Claims of all persons whatever. This deed is made subject to a deed heretofore made by me to John W. Hall, which deed conveyed a portion of a tract to me by the Will of my said husband. At the death of Mary Copeland the maker of this deed, I John C. Hall agree to see that she is buried beside her late husband, J. S. Copeland on the premises, This December 8th 1885.

Test

G. W. Carmack

Mary her x mark Copeland.

State of Tennessee }
Overton County } Personally appeared before me John Hart, clerk of the County Court for said County, Mary Copeland, the Conveyor, with whom I am personally acquainted, and who acknowledged that she executed the within deed for the purposes therein contained.

Witness my hand at Office this 8th day of December 1885,

John Hart, Clerk

The foregoing is a correct registration of a deed from Mary Copeland to John C. Hall and of the Certificate thereon. and was registered on 9th Dec. 1885. and filed in note book A. page 191. same day at 10. a.m.

J. W. Hammons Register

Letter written February 5, 1916 from Devol, Oklahoma
To The Golden Age, a local newspaper in Livingston, TN

Dear Sirs:

Will send you a few items from southwest Oklahoma

Been having lots of rainy, snowy, and icy weather, perhaps the worst winter of the nine I have been here. This weather is fine on our wheat. The ground is thoroughly thawed out so we can tell just how the wheat has come out of the freezing and it looks good. There is something like four out of every five acres that is in cultivation sowed to wheat and the country as a whole will average 120 acres in cultivation to the quarter section of 160 acres. So you can see we have quite a lot of wheat sowed in this country. Porter Worley, John W. Sweat and A. G. Norrod are in Oklahoma. Norrod and Sweat went to Elk City yesterday morning but will be back in a few days. They all seem to like the looks of our fine level and rich land. Also they like our friendly and intelligent people. They all seem astounded at what we have done in the last 8 or 9 years. It seems to them impossible for a country to be made up to date in that short time with nice residences barns and other out buildings and all the land in cultivation that needs to be inside so short a time. But we have the things to show and that is conclusive that we have them. Also our towns with water works and electric lights and them from 6 to 9 years old is a wonder to them. In talking about these things I told them that I had done on my land as much work and improvement put on as it would have taken three generations to have done in Tennessee. And I have the stuff to show to prove it. I have improved my Homestead and an Indian quarter section. So I have made two fine farms since coming here. Is not that the proof of what I have said? Devol will have a National Bank soon. There is a State Bank here now. All the Tennessee people are well. A. G. Norrod, J. W. Sweat, Porter Worley, D. G. Winningham, Mrs. D. G. Winningham, S. S. Morgan and I took dinner with S. A. Booher last Tuesday. Will close for this time.

Yours truly G. A. Smith

July 10, 1931

Willow Grove

Mrs. A. T. Donaldson of Celina R. 1 has accompanied her relatives Mr. and Mrs. Thacker back to Oklahoma for a several week's vacation.

Uncle Morgan Smith aged resident of the Celina R. 1 section died Sunday July 5 at three o'clock. He was a highly respected citizen of this community and is survived by his wife and a number of children. Interment was at the Ance Key graveyard.

Dr. Edward Clark of Willow Grove and Ned Davis of Celina had a car wreck near Hilham July 4 reports say that the small daughter of Dr. Clark is in a critical condition while others in Dr. Clark's car were injured although not quite so seriously. Mr. Davis received minor cuts and bruises his condition is not believed serious.

Mr. and Mrs. Dennis Thompson are the proud parents of a baby boy born July 5.

Mr. and Mrs. S. D. McClusky and Mrs. Sarah McClusky of Willow Grove were visiting Mr. and Mrs. W. D. Martin a short while ago.

October 1935

**CLAY COUNTY FARMER FOUND DEAD
AT FOOT OF BLUFF IN FARIVIEW
Community James L. Hogan 91 Had Been Missing Since
Sunday Night October 4th**
Left Son's Home Sat.

James L. Hogan 91 of the Willow Grove community of Clay County was found dead at the foot of a bluff in the Fairview community in Overton County, twelve miles north of Livingston early Wednesday morning. His body was discovered by Elliott Melton of Fairview. Mr. Hogan was last seen Sunday October 4th when he stopped about dark at the home of Mr. Melton and inquired as to a shorter route through the community to his home. He had left home Saturday to attend to some business in Overton County. Mr. Melton was attracted to the scene of the disaster by the unusual activity of birds and discovered the body lying face downward at the foot of the cliff. It is thought that due to darkness Mr. Hogan fell off the bluff resulting in his death. Mr. Hogan was a member of the Methodist Church South. He was an active farmer dealing in hogs cattle and grain. He was a former constable serving after he was 85 years old. At one time a number of years ago he was connected in business with William Hull father of Secretary of State Cordell Hull. He served in the Federal Army in 1865 in the War Between the States. Funeral services were held Wednesday at St. John's Cemetery at Willow Grove. He is survived by four sons G. Westley Hogan with whom he lived, Brinkley M. Hogan, J Frank Hogan all of Willow Grove and W. C. Hogan of Granite OK, one sister Mrs. Elizabeth Howard of Livingston one brother G. W. Morgan of Magnum OK, on nephew Dr. W. A. whole line illegible nephews Cato Taylor of Livingston, Dr. Harlan Taylor of Cookeville. His wife Mrs. Ella Maynord Hogan died in 1933 at the age of 93.

Early obituary tells of Cremation
Remains shipped to TN

Mrs. W. C. Robbins, Magaret Catherine [Sehon] Robbins dies in Colorado cremation service held remains to be shipped to Tennessee 1954.

Funeral services for Mrs. Margaret C. Robbins 76 who died at her home in Olathe Colo. At 10:25 a.m. December 11 after a long illness were held at 2 p.m. Monday in the chapel of Callahan Mortuary in Grand Junction Cremation followed with the remains to be shipped to Tennessee. Mrs. Robbins was the widow of the late Wylie C. Robbins well known Olathe building contractor who died June 20, 1953. Margaret Catherine Sehon was born October 10, 1877 at Livingston, Tenn. and spent her childhood in Tennessee. She was the daughter of Mr. and Mrs. James W. Sehon both deceased. She was married Mr. Robbins at Monterey, Tenn., December 27, 1907. The couple came to Olathe in September 1909 arriving the night before the opening of the Gunnison tunnel which brought the boom to this valley and made their home her the rest of their lives. As a contractor he had a role in the building of many homes and other structures in this area. The couple had no children Mrs. Robbins was a member of the Christian Science Church and of the American Legion Auxiliary. Surviving are her two sisters Mrs. Della Windle who came here form California more than a year ago to care for her sister and Mrs. Amy Roberson of Fallon Nev., five brothers Robert L. Sehon of St.Louis, John Sehon of Conroe, Tex., George W. and James Sehon of Salem, Ore., and William C. Shehon of Camp White, Ore.

Former Overton County residents return for visit after leaving over 50 years in later 1890's first visit in 50 years

Mr. Isaac D. Garrett of Oklahoma City his sister and husband Mr. and Mrs. Porter Gold and son of Muskogee, Okla., have been visiting Mr. and Mrs. Herman Eubank Mr. Isaac Garrett and Mrs. Gold were born in Overton County. They moved to Oklahoma with their parents when they were children. This is the first visit back here since they left here fifty years ago. Mr. Garrett and Mrs. Gold are children of the late Mr. and Mrs. Jay Garrett who once owned the old Garrett mill and the surrounding land. The visitors only found one old land mark the old Garrett barn and they also visited the family graveyard where their loved ones are resting.

Letter to Editor
Livingston Paper May 5 1952
Littlefield, Texas

April 22, 1952

The Enterprise

Gentlemen:

Please find enclosed $2.00 for which please send me your paper. I would be glad to see a few items from around Wirmingham, as that is where I was born and grew up to 20 years of age. My father's name was James Campbell Winningham. My mother's maiden name was Miss Clementine McDonald. She died in 1895 in Lampasas, county Texas. We came to Evant, Texas in 1894 and farmed on the Lampasas River for two years. Then in 1898 and 99 I went to school two years 5 miles west of Evant at a place called Fairview. In 1899-1900 I attended 9 months and received a first grade certificate but never did teach. I spent 15 months in the state on Montana returning to Texas where I married Miss Lizzy Ellen Smith the 10th day of November 1901. We have 5 children 2 boys and 3 girls all living 3 of them around 30 miles from us. I am not doing anything now except hoeing and picking cotton in the fall, 500 pounds and better per day. I have an uncle and lots of cousins and aunts supposed to be living near Wirmingham and I would be glad for them to write me sometime if they should see this in print. I wish I could go back there some time and I would love to see that dam they built on Obed River. I was baptized there by Bro. Jess Franklin in 1894 at the crossing going to the town of Byrdstown.

Yours Truly

M. H. Winningham

Author notes M.H. Winningham also known as Mack H. is on the 1900 census in Fergus County Montana age 26 being born in August 1874 in TN. Then on the 1910 Hale County Texas census married with children. He has many descendants and kin in Overton and Pickett Counties to this date.

September 3, 1917 Newspaper article
Bonita, Texas

I will write some news from Montague County, Texas in return form news from old Overton County Tenn. We receive our Enterprise on Tuesdays and always at our mail box waiting for it. We so much enjoy the letters from Allons, Hilham, Livingston and all other places.

I think the Enterprise is a good home paper and I think if everybody will do their part it can be made better. It now has good print and so why not let us do our bit and come on with the news from all parts of the country. We are having some fine weather now with the big dews at night. Health is good; we had a big rain Sunday August 19, which insures fine crap grass for winter pasture. Our corn crop is very light but in most cases people will have enough to do them the early corn will soon do to gather and most of the June corn is in roasting ears and is fine. Cotton is an average crop so far and looks like it might make one third bale to the acre, beginning to open some, Cotton sack duck is 25cents a yard against 12 ½ cents last year ginning $5 bale, future contracts on seed $50 to $ 60 a ton and cotton 20 cents a pound it may bring more than that, but I believe there will be more cotton raised than some are expecting. Peanuts are looking fine and they are easy to raise and easy harvested. They are taking the place of cotton in a hurry. Here is the reason for that; Say a farmer planted one hundred acres to peanuts and say he will make at a very low figure for an example, fifty tons of hay at $20 to $25 a ton and twenty to twenty five bushels of peanuts per acre at $1.25 bushel; so you figure up and see how and why peanuts are taking the place of cotton. Early feed is good and late feed looking well. A good peach crop is on and drying and can and canning fruit is now in order. Green Cook is on a boom making sweet "lasses" most everybody will have some made this time. Cull Reeves was down here on a real estate business trip a few days ago. Uncle Jack Sidwell says he is thinking of going to Tennessee some time soon. My letter is getting to long, so I'll quit now.

Albert L. Morgan

Author's notes additional information 1920 census for Montague Co. TX shows Albert Morgan age 34 born in TN with wife Missie born in TN then 6 children also living in the household as a lodger was Curtis Johnson age 40 m born in TN, In 1910 Census Albert was still living in Overton Co. TN in district 3rd with wife Missie and 3 children. I have more information on this family also.

A Tribute of Respect

The death angels visited the home of W.M. Burgess on Jan. the 24th 1918 and claimed his companion, Addie. Addie was born Feb. 28th, 1888. She professed religion at 16 years of age and joined the Baptist Church at Fellowship and has lived a devoted Christian life. She was loved by all who knew her. She leaves a husband and three small children, the youngest being about 2 years of age. She was buried at Fellowship the 26th. Funeral services being conducted by Rev. Dickens. The berieved family has our sympathy.

A friend

Author's additional information Addie was before marriage Addie Maynard and W. M. Burgess was William Martin Burgess.

Family and Kin Reunion
August 1925

On Sunday August 2nd a family reunion was given near the home of Mr. and Mrs. T. C. Clark on the river in what is known as Duncan's Bottom in honor of MR. Clark's niece Mrs. S. M. Beene and son Melvin Beene and her daughter Mrs. T.N. Soddox and two sons Leon and T.N. all of Harrison Ark. The following who were present to enjoy the day were Mrs. S.M. Beene and son, Mrs. T.N. Shaddox and two sons, of Ark., Mr. and Mrs. T.C. Clark, Mrs. S.B. Harward and children, W. D. Clark and family, of Livingston Mrs. Fount Arney Mrs. Eddie Mullions and family Henry Murphy and family Dr. and Mrs. Clark and Mr. and Mrs. Bob Clark of Willow Grove Mrs. and Mrs. Clark of Lillydale Mr. and Mrs. Frank Roberts Mr. and Mrs. Joe Porter Harrison and daughter Mrs. Susan Harrison and daughter Mrs. Albert Clark Mr. and Mrs. Turner Clark Mr. and Mrs. Ellen Jewett Mrs. Clark Arney Mrs. Hoy Arney Mr. and Mrs. Crit Arney Benton Hapkins and family Miss Larkie Clark of Lillydale Mr. and Mrs. Ras Clark and daughter of Oakley Mr. and Mrs. Ed Hargrove of Willow Grove Mr. and Mrs. Walter Cross Mr. and Mrs. Jolly. About

12 o'clock the table was spread and filled to its limit with all kinds of delicious and appetizing foods some remarked that the table didn't look like a drouth. Everyone enjoyed the dinner and the association together as they all knew just the same thing would never happen again. Pictures were made of the crowd of about 125. About 4 o'clock all went away feeling happy over the day but sad over parting. May God Bless our gathering together and keep us true to Him until we meet at that great reunion with Him on high.

COUPLE REMARRY AT ALLONS
AFTER BEING SEPARATED 50 YEARS

August 1936

The wedding of Mrs. Edna Noe and Wiliam Abbett which took place on last Monday July 27, at the residence of Rev. John M. Brown who officiated was one of unusual interest to a wide circle of relatives and friends because of the romance it carries. The bride is the daughter of the late Mr. and Mrs. Andy Burgess and who was born and reared near Livingston. The bridegroom is a native of Wayne County Kentucky. They met and married on May 7, 1881 at the home of the bride's parents under the name of Miss Permelia E. Burgess and William A. Abbett with Rev. J. C. Jackson a well known Baptist minister officiating. This marriage was held sacred for some eight years and three children were born two daughters and one son were born to them. Discord arose resulting in a separation and a divorce. Mr. Abbett returning to his native Kentucky where he married a second wife and reared a family of several children. Mrs. Abbett remained in the community of her childhood and was subsequently married to Mr. Noe who died a few months ago. Mr. Abbett's Kentucky wife having died also he returned to Tennessee to find his first love and they were remarried after a separation of 50 years. At the time of their first marriage the bride was 17 and groom was 22 at their second marriage the bride is 72 and the groom is 77. First love although surpressed for a half century has been rekindled and will doubtless brighten the remainder of life's journey until they reach the end of the way. "All is well that ends well"

Obituary from February 1915

Mrs. Angeline Terry

Mrs. Angeline Abigall Campbell Terry was the daughter of Samuel and Lucinda (Fiske) Denton and was born June 13, 1827 near Sparta White County Tennessee near what is known as the Rock House and would have been 88 next June. She died at the residence of her daughter Mrs. Lucy Mitchell Jan. 22, 1915 after a brief illness. She was the younger of two children both girls her older sister Sarah having married Ormel Fiske the father of the writer and died at Hilham in September 1892 at the age of about 68. Samuel Denton their father was a native of New Jersey and came to this state about the year 1803 and settled in White County. Their mother was a native of New Braintree, Massachustts, and came to Overton County in 1803 with her parents who settled near Hilham when she was only about three years old. Mrs. Terry was twice married her first husband being Robert C. Burton by whom she had two children twin boys William and Samuel Denton Burton, Will died when a child and S. D. Burton now lives in the state of Oklahoma. After the death of her first husband she married Elijah W. Terry by whom she had the following children, now living Mrs. Emma Burgess, of R.1 Sparta, Tenn. Mrs. Lucy I. Mitchell wife of R.L. Mitchell Jr. of Livingston, Tenn., Mrs. Celina V. Dever of Endee, N.M., Adrian M. Terry of Clyne Park, Mont., R. Y. Terry of Magnum, Okla., At the time of her marriage to E. W. Terry he had six children by a former wife who had died to wit. James W. Terry, W. L. Terry, Jesse Terry, Julia now the wife of John Cook of Hilham, Rettie the wife of Thomas Lynn of Cookeville, Elizabeth who married Burt Johnson and died leaving three children. Mrs. Terry was noted for untiring energy and her high purpose and goodness of heart. It seemed a part of her mission in life to look after those in need or distress, and she made it her business to see that those needing help got it. She was a great worker woman of superior sense and ability and had well defined and fixed ideals of her own, which she lived up to the best her surroundings allowed. She had a high sense of honor and despised a liar or dishonest person. She was kind and hospitable to all who went about her being lavish in providing for the wants of her guests, and kind and motherly to all so she won and kept the love and esteem of her step-children who loved her almost as though she were their own mother.

She became a member of the Christian church at an early age and although not a frequent church goer, she lived a practical Christian life there by proving her faith by her works. Her life was an application of the cardinal principles of Christianity void of empty show and hollow pretense but alive and aglow with good deeds strewn all along her life's pathway. Although she was a very earnest woman full of purpose and push she was also a jovial and fun loving disposition mingling mirth with the work and duties of each day. Nor did age dim her sunny temperament or render her petulant or childish. Even almost to the day of her death although very deaf and nearly blind she retained her cheerful spirit going about singing the songs of her youth and caring for herself in a great measure because as she said she did not wish to be of trouble to anyone. For several years prior to her death her memory of passing events we faulty so that she could not retain recent occurrences but her mind was otherwise apparently unimpaired and she loved to dwell upon the scenes of the past. She was whole souled and thorough going in all her ways and whatever she did she did with all her might. Her husband died in 1900 and she remained at the old home place and lived with a tenant until about a year ago when after repeated persuasions she yielded to the request of her daughter Mrs. Lucy Mitchell and went to Livingston where she remained until her death. Mrs. Lucy Mitchell Mrs. Julia Cook and Mrs. Emma Burgess were the only children with her during her last illness. She was buried at Smyrna near her old home in Putnam county. She yearned to die after losing her hearing and sight saying she was ready to go at any time and that she did not believe it wrong to desire to go. If one reaps as one has sown and there is Elysium where tired and weary souls go and are at rest to meet with loved ones gone before after this life's fitful glow then we believe our dear old aunt has gone to that happy land.

W.D. Fiske in Celina Bugle

OVERTON NATIVES PAY FIRST VISIT IN 59 YEARS

October 1956

Mr. and Mrs. Bill Miller of Colbert, Oklahoma and their daughter and her husband, Mr. and Mrs. Gene Coleman of Bristow, Oklahoma, were recent visitors I Livingston and Overton county. Mrs. Miller is the former Delia Hensley and left Tennessee with her parents the late Elbert and Jane Hensley 59 years ago. Mr. Miller moved west from near Albany, Ky 71 years ago. It was the first time either one had been back. It was Mr. and Mrs. Colemans first visit to this section. On Sunday Oct., 14 Mrs. J. H. Sells sister of Mrs. Miller gave a dinner at her home for the visitors which was attended by about twenty relatives and friends. Several other called during the afternoon. On Saturday and again on Monday the visitors wer house guests of Mr. and Mrs. Albert Hensley of Route 5. Mr. Hensley is Mrs. Miller nephew. They Saturday dinner guests of Mr. and Mrs. Lee Hensley of Route 1 Monroe and on Monday they visited Mrs. Lucy Holman Route 2 Mr. and Mrs. R. L. Sells and Mrs. Nannie Richardson Ozone community and Mrs. Tillie Clark of Allons Route 1.

From Pierce City, MO.
May 23rd 1899

Miss Hattie Qualls

Windle Tenn.

My dear precious neice Your very kind and nice letter of May 11th was received by due course of mail and read by us with much interest. I was glad to get a letter from one of sister Renies children.

It was so well written and so full of news, I was so glad to hear from you all even if it did give some sad news I had just a few days before got a letter form Mrs. Martha Pickett of Cookeville informing me of sister Martha Henrys death on May 6th and that a Mr. Allgood was the executor of her will. I would like to know who she willed her estate to. I hope she remembered you all in her will. Wells I was so sorry to learn that your precious dear mothers health continues so feeble I would be so glad to see her and your pa and their dear children but this I reckon will be and impossibility in this life first my health is too feeble I will be seventy three years old 23rd day of next June an confined to my home am quite feeble not able to preach any have been in the active ministry since 1850 but feel like my work is about done on earth. Second I have not the means to spare to come to see you all if well enough. You asked me to send you my picture I have not got a good one on hand. I will send you one when I have some taken. I was glad to learn you were all Christians and lovers of Jesus the Savior of sinners. He has been precious to me for over fifty six years the same old religion I got at Shiloh has kept me all these long years yes the same Lord Jesus my strength in youth my support in manhood my comfort in old age this is my testimony for him tried under all circumstances in life's troubles He has sustained me I know religion will do as I have proved and ___ tried it. If we are children of God the name we are known by here matters but little Methodist, Baptist, or Cumberland Presbyterian, yet Cumberland Presbyterian sounds sweetest to me. I suppose this is natural to all to love the family name some the best. You spoke of your Pa's family that there were six living children and five dead so we must all died sooner or later. My fathers family is nearly all gone there were ten children father and mother Renie, Minda, and myself only remain out the family of twelve. It seems as but a few days ago when the twelve was all at our old home and together constituted a happy home among the mountains of Tennessee. The scenes of my boyhood days linger in my memory today the mountains the valleys the roads the trees that cover the land. The refreshing clear cool springs so numerous where I used to quench my thirst these are things I cannot forget. The old friends of my boyhood days. I suppose are nearly all dead. It makes me feel rather lonesome it seems that I have out lived most of my generation. In reviewing my life I feel like I have done the best I could for the up lift of humanity and the bettering of our race I have witnessed about five thousand conversion to Christ taken over three thousand into the church a number of these have made ministers of the gospel and are doing a good work yet I wish I could have done more and better work for the Masters cause than I have but I feel that my work is well nigh finished and that I am getting near the door of my eternal Home where the wicked cease from troubling and the weary are at rest. This scattering letter is intended not only for you but for all the family a few words especially to your mother the Bible says "All things work together for good to them that love God Rom. 8:28" Hence these afflictions and to refine us again another good promise these affections shall work our a far more and eternal weight of glory another precious text is St. John 14th the whole chapter is precious to me and then the 23rd Psalm. May the Lord bless you dear sister and give you grace according to your day and need. Dear niece write again soon. This leaves us both in bad health the Lord bless you. Your affectionate Uncle

M. C. Miller

Additional genealogy to go along with the above letter, M. C. is McCormick Miller according the Lawrence County Missouri 1900 census Pierce City, McCormick Miller age 73 born June 1826 in TN occupation preacher he had been married 44 years wife listed was Harriet C. age 67 born August 1832 in TN listed she had 3 children with only 1 living. Hattie Qualls was born June 1879 in TN daughter of Thomas Qualls born May 1829 in TN married 45 years wife was Cyrena born February 1832 listed she had 10 children with only 5 living other children known are Riley, Sallie, Mary and Hattie this information was taken from 1900 census Overton County TN. Cyrena [Miller] Qualls and McCormick Miller were brothers and sisters.

ALPINE WOMAN CELEBRATES 100TH BIRTHDAY

March 1948

On March 9th Mrs. Martelia Ledford celebrated her one hundredth birthday at the home of P.L. Carlock of Alpine where she lives with her daughter Mrs. P. L. Carlock. Several friends and relatives called on her during the day. Among those who came form a distance were her son Loyd Shepard; granddaughter Mrs. Reece Haney; grandson Bernard Shepard great granddaughter Joyce Ann Shepard all of Arkansas. Mrs. Ledford has survived two husbands her first husband Logan Shepard died early in their marriage. Two children survive from that marriage Mrs. Laura Robbins Seattle Wash., and Loyd Shepard of Forum Arkansas. Her second marriage was to Francis M. Ledford who died in 1938 in 1932 Mr. and Mrs. Ledford celebrated their Golden Anniversary. Two children from their union are still living Mrs. P. L. Carlock of Alpine and Elmer Ledford of Oak Grove. In addition to these four living children Mrs. Ledford has twenty five grandchildren thirty eight great grandchildren and four great great grandchildren. Mrs. Ledford took the day with its excitement rather quietly during much of the talk around her she looked from person to person as if trying to place all the faces. Because of hearing difficulties she does not enter readily into conversation but she retains a lively interest in people and events. She has no physical inability other than a lack of balance in walking which causes her to use a stick. She has regular habits which include going to bed at 4 o'clock in the winter drinking a large glass of water before breakfast and eating an egg for breakfast every morning. She reads without glasses her reading material is chiefly the Bible although she likes to look at the Enterprise and the daily paper. She writes to a few people regularly but cannot keep up a steady correspondence with all of her grandchildren who write her. Mrs. Ledford's favorite Bible quotation is the one beginning "In my father's house are many mansions...." and she feels that one is prepared for her there.

A. S. J. DAUGHERTY DIES IN ARKANSAS

May 1934

Albert Sidney Daugherty 69 of Fort Smith Ark. Died at his home where had lived for the past thirty years after an illness of several months duration. He had been a traveling salesman for many years and was forced to quit active life by reason of failing health. He had also been engaged in the real estate business as a side-line and was a popular and successful business man. He was born at Livingston and educated here leaving here after he reached adult age. His ancestors were pioneers of this section and were noted for their valor and courage among the early settlers. His grandfather Cornelius Daugherty who was a strong character and his paternal grandmother was of the Hamilton family who settled at Bennett's Ferry on Cumberland river. His father was Colonel Ferdinand Hamilton Daugherty who served as Colonel in the Confederate Army during the War Between the States and was an active character in the affairs in Overton County and Livingston for a half century prior to his death a few years ago. Before Civil War he was an active successful merchant. Subsequent to the war he practiced law was for many years an active member of the County Court and was register of deeds at the time of his death. His mother's maiden name was Mary Snodgrass who was a native of White County and a member of one of the most prominent families of the state. His father was a first cousin to Colonel Oliver Hamilton who was captured by the Federal soldiers and murdered in 1864. He was twice married first to Miss Maggie Snodgrass of White County. Some time after her death he married Miss Jennie Stroud of Arkansas who survives. To this union were born two sons A.S.J. Jr. and James Ferdinand Daugherty who survive. The former is engaged in the lumber business and the latter is a law pupil in the University at Fayetteville, Ark. He is also survived by two brothers ___ A. Daugherty of Nashville and H. Colquitt Daugherty of St. Louis and two sisters Mrs. Sibba D. Chapin and Mrs. Sallie D. Lewis of Memphis, also by a stepmother Mrs. Laura C. Daugherty and two half sisters Mrs. Enna D. Kelly of

Lubbock, Texas and Mrs. Mary Hancock of New Mexico and three half brothers Benton M., Ferdinand H. and Grover C. Daugherty all of San Antonio Texas.

Alabama Letter

Golden Age Article February 1920

A few lines from this city might be of interest to some of my old friends. I look with pleasure to the coming of the Golden Age every Saturday I see the names of many of my old friends in your paper. I have in Alabama since 1887 but I have made several trips back to my old home above Monroe. I had the pleasure of spending the 4th of July last summer in Livingston and met up with many of my old friends and school mates. I am proud to see old Overton County is pressing forward in boys corn clubs and other progressive lines. I notice the advocating of some money crop. I am sure that you could plant a few acres of cotton at present price and make big money as it is worth lint and seed about $230.00 bale and here in Gadsen on some prize acres two bales is produced per acre or $460 per acre by selecting early varieties and using 400 or 500 lbs of fertilizer per acre. Cotton would make a good crop up there as I remember seeing it grow as high as my head on my father's old farm and there is no danger of the bowl weevil up there for years yet. We have had very mild winter down here have had no snow and but little ice. If I see this in print will try again sometime.

R. A. Wright

Gadsen, Ala.

Author's additional information on Wright family R. A. is Robert Anthony Wright born 24 July 1863 in Overton County TN and died 23 August 1921 Etowah Alabama son of Rufus Washingston and Minervia Jane [Burtram] Wright many descendants still live in Overton and Pickett Counties today.

Early picture of the Rufus Washington Wright old home place at Wirmingham Community in Overton County TN where Robert Anthony R. A. Wright was writing about in the previous letter in 1920 from Gadsen, Alabama.

Front row, left to right is Fred Wright, Rufus Washington Wright, Cora, Sara, June, John M. Wright, Mrs. John M. Wright, Bill Wright. Back row, left to right, is Noah Wright, Mrs. Noah Wright, A. M. Wright, Martilla, Grant Wright.

December 9, 1897 Article

Non-Resident Notice.

Petition to Sell Land.

J. N. Cannon, et als. } In this cause it appearing from the petition that defendants Andrew France a resident of the State of Missouri, James Burl France, a minor, and his regular Guardian, James Robinson, Mary Wright and her husband J. L. Wright, and Sam Buck, residents of the State of Texas, and John France whose residence is unknown to complainants and cannot be ascertained after diligent inquiry, are all non-residents of the State of Tennessee, or of unknown residences, so that the ordinary process of law cannot be served upon them: It is, therefore, ordered that publication be made in the Overton County Enterprise, a news paper published in Livingston, Tenn., for four consecutive weeks, commanding said above named defendants to appear at the January Term of the County Court for Overton County, to be held in the town of Livingston, Overton County, Tenn., on Monday the 6th day of Jan. 1898, to plead, answer or demur to complainants bill, or the some will be taken for confessed as to them and the cause set for hearing exparte.

This Nov. 26th 1897.

R. L. Mitchell Jr. Clerk.

Officer & Roberts, Sols. 12 2 4t.

Central Gazzette June 17 1843
State of Tennessee
Overton County February Tem of the Circuit Court 1843
Article Below

Early divorce of Thomas Whitworth VS Juda Whitworth

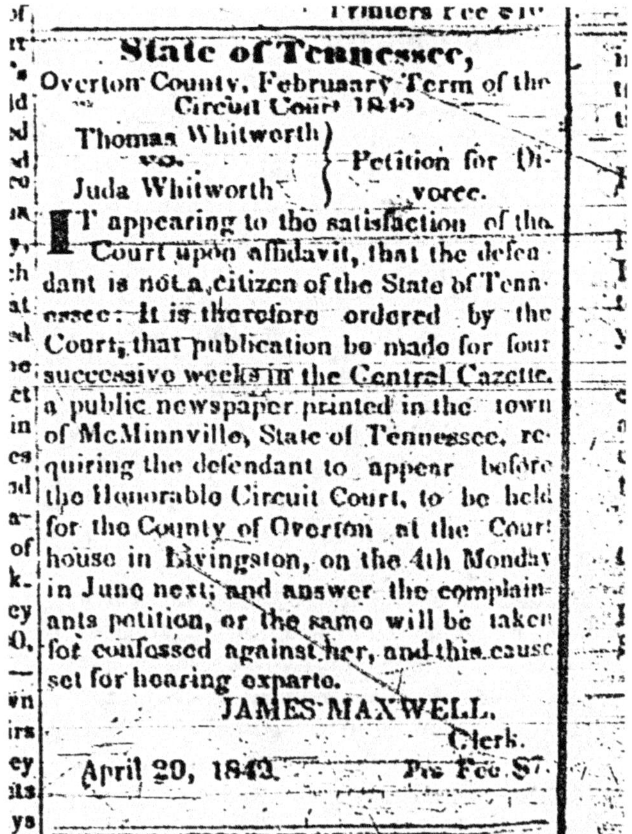

State of Tennessee,

Overton County, February Term of the Circuit Court 1843

Thomas Whitworth
   vs.   } Petition for Divorce.
Juda Whitworth

IT appearing to the satisfaction of the Court upon affidavit, that the defendant is not a citizen of the State of Tennessee: It is therefore ordered by the Court, that publication be made for four successive weeks in the Central Gazette, a public newspaper printed in the town of McMinnville, State of Tennessee, requiring the defendant to appear before the Honorable Circuit Court, to be held for the County of Overton at the Court house in Livingston, on the 4th Monday in June next, and answer the complainants petition, or the same will be taken for confessed against her, and this cause set for hearing exparte.

JAMES MAXWELL,
Clerk.

April 20, 1843.

Additional information on Juda Whitworth below

1850 Census Overton Co TN Dist#4/396-396Francis Jennings 37 m NC farmer; Sara 35 f KY; William 13 m TN; Ezekial 11m TN; Susan 8 f TN; Martha 6 f TN; Ambrose 2 m TN; Judah Whitworth 66 f VA

Obituary February 10, 1933

JOHN N. COX DIES IN TEXAS FRIDAY OF HEART ATTACK
Native of Overton County Descendant of Early Settlers here
Many Relatives Here

John N. Cox 83 died Friday at his home in Sulphur Springs, Texas of a heart attack. He had been in town Friday evening in his usual good health and was stricken a few hours later. He was a native of Overton county having been born in Bates Cove in that part of the Martin Cox 600 acre entry which fell to his father Enoch Cox. Martin Cox was one of the pioneer settlers coming from East Tennessee then North Carolina and settling three and one-half miles east of Livingston in 1806. John N. Cox's father was married to Miss Margaret McMillin who was familiarly called Peggy in 1849. To this union were born seven children John N. Cox the eldest was born in 1850, His father enlisted as a volunteer in the confederate army and served until the surrender in the spring of 1865. On account of his cool judgment and courage and being a crack shot he was frequently assigned to hazardous detail service. The war over he returned to his devastated farm and began the work of making a crop but was forced to abandon this undertaking on account of abuses and threats to take his life by Federal guerillas who had not yet laid down arms. Being advised by friends that he was in constant danger of losing his life he left in the summer of 1865 for the west and spent a short while in Missouri thence to Texas where he died in 1867. John N. Cox then fifteen had incurred the enmity which was followed by threats from the guerilla outlaws also left that same fall to join his father in the west. He after spending some time in Missouri and Arkansas made his permanent home in Hopkins County. He soon became prominent in the affairs of the county serving six years as assistant County Court Clerk and eight years as County Court Clerk of Hopkins County. He married there to Miss Florence Lindley and became a familiar figure. It was said in the Hopkins County Echo that there has never been a man in Hopkins County who came nearer knowing every man woman and child in Hopkins County nor one who was known and loved by a greater number of people than John N. Cox. Another paying tribute to him in the same paper said "My friend has crossed the Great Divide and while I do not know whether he was a member of any church or not yet we firmly believe that having acted kind sympathetic and charitable in this world that in the mystic circle to which he now belongs that peace and happiness will be his allotted portion". He was a Democrat and a member of the I.O.O.F. The mother and six other children two boys and four girls procured an ox wagon covered and left with scant rations for the west in 1868 to join the subject of this sketch. Although quite young the writer remembers John N. Cox and his family and every member of the family. Many of the older citizens of this community who knew him will learn of his death with regret. He has many relatives in Tennessee among whom are John M. Smith of Alpine, H. Alex Smith of Livingston, James M. Cox of Carthage, Hicks Cox of Dixon Springs, first cousins to him. James W. Henson and Mrs. Mary Etta Myers of Livingston and Mrs. Sophronia Mitchell of Crossville, are also near relatives. Elder Thomas Stover of Crossville is also a first cousin of the deceased. He is survived by his wife Mrs. Florence Cox and one daughter Miss Myrtle Cox of Sulphur Springs Texas and a sister f Missouri.

FAMILY REUNION HELD LAST SATURDAY
Article July 1931

At the old home in the Sinking Cane a fertile farming section on the southeastern portion of Overton county some four miles North of the Town of Monterey where A. J. Walker Sr. and his wife Mrs. Clemmie Verble Walker began their young life soon after their marriage 85 years ago and where they each lived until overtaken by death there was held last Saturday a very happy family reunion. The former passed away in the year 1913 at the age of 89 years and the latter died in the year 1910 at the age of 79 years. Theirs was an unusually long union and a most happy one as well as a most successful one. There were born to this union fourteen children, five sons and nine daughters all living to adult age. Twelve are living and eleven were able to join each other in the reunion last Saturday at the old home where they spent their childhood Mrs. Ora Andrews wife of P. Andrews resident of the state of Texas was not able to attend. Those attending were as follows.

Jas. C. Walker of Monterey, Wm. H. Walker of Hartsville, A.J. Walker Jr. of Cumberland County, Kentucky Jos. B. Walker of Celina Susan W. Ray widow of George N. Ray of Monterey Mrs. Hennie W. Copeland widow of A. C. Copeland of Beaver Hill Mrs. Lee Ann McCormack widow of Wm. McCormack of Algood Mrs. Kate W. Terry wife of Roland Terry of Celina Mrs. Hallie Walker of Monterey Mrs. Lou Matthews of Livingston and Mrs. Belle W. Lea wife of G. Wash Lea of Livingston Besides the near relatives almost the entire community as well as many friends from Clay, Putnam, Jackson, White and Cumberland counties were there. The number attending has been conservatively estimated at from five to six hundred people The reunion had been widely advertised and ample preparations made for a good time the weather was fine and a full day was enjoyed by all. The immediate family prepared fatted pigs and lambs and chickens galore with all sorts of breads and cookies. At the noon hour devotional exercises were led by Rev. A. T. Judkins pastor of the Celina Circuit followed by all taking a part in the serving of refreshments which was done with more or less premeditation and forethought until every one was satisfied fully. The founder of the home above described was the outstanding figure in the vicinity in which he spent an unusually long life. He had been blessed mentally and physically and was active to the day of his death to the extent of having done a days plowing the day he died. He led a temperate life and was devoted to home and family and was a kind and accommodating neighbor religiously he was a Methodist and politically a Democrat.

September 1898

Albert France's wife ne-Miss Hannah Hartsoe, died Saturday and was buried at Liberty in the Deck Cove Sunday. She left twin boys only three days old and a husband to mourn her departure with a host of friends and relatives to whom we tender condolence.

The funeral of Campbell Ramsey and wife and Chambers Ramsey will be preached at Falling Springs Church the first Sunday in October 1898 by W. S. Guthrie and Smith Grider.

August 23 1935

KIMES FAMILY REUNION

For the first time in a period of several years the children of the late A. P. Kimes five daughters and four sons were together in a family reunion at the Kimes home near Allred Sunday. Those present were Mrs. and Mrs. Willis Kimes, Mrs. Clyde Kimes, of Clarkrange, Curtis Kimes and daughter Clara, Aren Kimes, Nora Kimes, Pearl Kimes, Mrs. Ella Copeland, Mrs. and Mrs. J. A. Richards and daughter Lerion of Allred, Tilber Kimes and daughters Etta and Lee, Mrs. Joe S. Flannigan and Mr. Flannigan and little James Ussery of Columbia, Mr. and Mrs. Walter Oakley and children, Irene, Dois, Eugene and Ronald of Rickman, Mr. and Mrs. Joe Swack and daughters Golda and Auda Marie and Uncle Jim Swack, (only living uncle of the family) of Monterey. Other near relatives not present were Mrs. Christine Ussery of Columbia, Kimes and Ulrie Oakley of Rickman, Mrs. Albert Ray of Livingston, and Mrs. Joel Parrott of Tipton Oklahoma.

Oxen Were Used Many Years Ago

Oren Vaughn and Albert Ramsey in front, others unknown
Notice the large wood yoke attached to oxen.

Jim & Becky Qualls, caretakers of the county home in Overton County for many years. After Jim's death, Becky did it for several years.

L-R Lee Stephens, Sallie Holder, Minnie Savage, Rhodie Ledbetter.
Picture made at last County Home, which was located on County
House Road in Livingston.

Louis Swafford holding chicken. Notice all the other people in background with chickens in crates and the sign over the door. Chickens were bought and sold and shipped by train.

Standing by wagon is Tillman and Julia (Qualls) Ledbetter
Others are relatives also.

Left to Right, Florence (Allred) Cantrell, with Bill, Kirby, Kelly
(Cantrell) Stout, Ridley Stout, Albert, Lorimer, baby is Coy
(Stout) Swafford

John Porter Bilbrey, born 2 Sep 1847 died 7 Apr 1924, buried
Wm. Bilbrey Cemetery. Overton Co Sheriff 1873-76

Martelia (Deck) Bilbrey, born 25 Feb 1857 died 30 Mch 1942 Wife
of John Porter Bilbrey, Buried Wm Bilbrey Cemetery.

William C. Martin old tintype photograph born 23 Feb 1843
died 13 Jan. 1912, buried Dan Martin Cemetery

Joe D. Hatcher old tintype photograph

A Sad Letter From Washington
June 1917 Article

Hoquiam, Wash.,
May 17, 1917

Dear Father and Mother

With sad feelings and broken heart I'll write you a few lines. This leaves me in the saddest frame of mind ever in life. Yesterday at 5:45 p.m. my brother Tom was killed by a train. He was braking on a log train. I'll send the clipping out of the paper. I wasn't with him. I was about twenty miles from where he got killed. I cannot bring him home I can tell you more when I get there. I think I'll start for home in four or five days. I'll do the best I can with the body and give him the best burial possible. He is now in the hands of the undertakers. So I'll close. From your son.

Ed Richardson

Clipping from paper:

Tom H. Richardson a brakeman on the Polson Logging Railway was instantly killed about 5:45 last evening when he fell in front of the cars on which he was riding and the left hand tracks of 22 cars passed over him, his body being cut practically in two a short distance above the waist. The accident was witnessed by W. Grace of Hoquiam, another brakeman on the same train. The engine hauling 22 empty cars were on a down grade about a quarter of a mile this side of the railroad camp made a flying switch to set the empties out. Richardson cut the train loose and stayed on the head car to set the brakes while Grace stayed with the engine and dropped off to turn the switch. Owing to the fact that they were on a down grade and had been moving at a rapid rate of speed the cars jerked heavily as Richardson applied the brakes and he was thrown forward losing his grasp on the brake and falling across the rails in front of the cars. W. Grace saw his comrade killed he was only about 100 feet ahead of the cars at the switch. The body was gathered up as soon as possible and

C. C. Pinnick was notified. The body is at the Pinnick Undertaking Parlors, awaiting funeral arrangements Tom H. Richardson was 30 years of age and was single. One brother D. E. Richardson is employed at Polson Camp No. 8 other relatives living in Livingston Tenn., have been notified. Deceased came to Washington last July and started work in Polson Camp where he had been employed since. He had been promoted to the position of brakeman on the logging train only a week ago.

Byrd Gore and Willie Matthews
Windle TN community about 1915

Rebecca (Flowers) Wright

Shown feeding little chickens at home in the Wirmingham Community of Overton County. She was born 3 November 1862 in Overton Co. TN, died 1 July 1956. She was the daughter of Simon H. & Margaret (Smith) Flowers. She was married to "J.M." Wright in Overton Co. TN 19 July 1891.

J. M. Wright was born 19 July 1858 in Overton Co. TN died 24 January 1938. He was son of Rufus Washington and Minerva Jane (Bertram) Wright.

This family was in the General Merchandise business in Overton County years ago in the Wirmingham Community where they lived. There are many people living today that descend from this family in Pickett and Overton Counties.

Isaac Newton "Newt" Poston

He was the son of Solomon "Babe" and Elizabeth "Betsy" (Duke) Poston. He was born 18 January 1852 died 9 September 1940 and is buried in the Zion Hill Cemetery in Overton County TN. He had 9 siblings, to name them are

John Franklin, J Townsend, Richard, William, Leanna (Poston) Williford, Odecia (Poston) Yelton, Martelia "Teal" (Poston) Peek, Nebraska "Brass" Poston, Minnesota "Mint" Poston.

Minnesota "Mint" Poston
She was born August 1858 died June 1932

Robert "Pool" Yelton born 5 October 1847 died 6 September 1913 buried Paran Cemetery in Overton County TN. He was husband of Odecia (Poston) and son of Charles L. and Edith (Norris) Yelton.

Odecia (Poston) Yelton

Some Family History
By E. F. Christian

The romance of Nancy Shultz Fisk my great grandmother born 1803 married to Moses Fiske 1823. The elder Fiske came to New York City from England later moved to New Hampshire and Massachusetts. Moses Fiske a graduate of Dartmouth College and Yale University came to Tennessee in 1799. The Fiske were a family of educators and professional people Moses Fiske was dean of Dartmouth College for a time. Educator, Mathematician, surveyor and early pioneer of Overton County. The State Historical Society erected a plaque on his honor in front of the old Fiske home ¼ mile W. of Hilham on Cookeville road.

In the state line dispute between North Carolina, Ky and Tennessee the U.S. Government called on Dartmouth College for her best surveyor and mathematician. Moses Fiske was one of the three selected to make the survey the three were also appointed a committee of three to divide the state of N. Carolina the eastern half to remain the state of N. Carolina and the western became the state of Tennessee.

The entire state boundary of N. Carolina was surveyed and the sate divided the eastern half N. Carolina the western half becoming Tennessee. Moses Fiske received large land grants for his services (a three year work) he settled in N. Overton County where he built the first female college south of the Mason-Dixie line and later established an academy for boys. Several of the Fiske students later acquired national prominence. Later Moses Fiske established colonies in Overton, Clay and Putnam counties. These colonies were established approximately 10 miles distance from each other. Some of the surviving ones are Hilham, Cookeville, Livingston what is now Burristown and Celina named for his daughter Celina Fiske (my grandmother) and some others tht failed to survive.

Nancy Shultz my great grandmother Legend Nancy Shultz one of the early colonists a pioneer beauty of sweet sixteen accompanied by a small brother had to make a 20 mile journey to another colony to buy garden seed for her colony. She stopped at the home of Moses Fiske toask for a drink of water for the child. They had carried lunch with them and wouldn't dine with bachelor Fiske but he made a date with young Nancy to have dinner with him the following day at his house on their return trip which she did. Moses was very much enamored of the young beauty and dated her to have dinner with her the following Sunday at her home.

Moses Fisk home as it stands today located at Standing Stone State Park on a hill just above one lane bridge.

On arriving at the Shultz home he found everything so neat and clean the yard swept clean the floors scrubbed white with sand the beds and furnishings all spic and span every chair stool and shelf covered with a white clean cloth the whole house immaculately clean and sweet and an excellent dinner well cooked and served and Nancy so exoticly sweet and beautiful that he completely lost his heart right then and there. He asked father Shultz permission to pay his respects to the fair Nancy which was granted and then asked for the fair lady's hand in marriage which was also granted.

On being informed by Mr. Shultz that Nancy had no education asked that he may educate her before they married which was also agreed to. He told his prospective father in law that he was ambitious to raise a large family and the he wanted the mother of his children to be an educated woman. So he sent his bride to be to Dartmouth College for four years at his own expense. He never saw Nancy for three years at the end of four years he brought his bride to the home that he had prepared for her and they were married in the old Fisk home now standing occupied and in good repair. Nancy was twenty years old then.

They raised a large family and lived to a ripe old age and are buried at the Fiske cemetery near their home at Hilham, Tenn.

Early Divorces in Overton Co. TN
Before 1870

This information was taken form various court record books and loose records located in Overton County. I have individual files on some of these divorces records that is the complete the below information below is only extracts from the source. Some of these books are on microfilm.

October Term 1847 Catherine Laley VS William H. Laley petition for divorce they married in Overton Co. TN in 1846.

George W. Garrett VS Dianah Garrett they married in Overton Co. TN 9 January 1842 Diniah maiden name was Hill before marriage she left in 1845 George is a citizen of Benton Co. TN.

Elizabeth Odle VS Berry Odle bill for divorce married about 16 years ago she is a resident of Overton Co. and Berry is a resident of Jackson Co. TN.

Silas Copeland VS Dicy (Phillips) Copeland petition for divorce they were married in Overton Co. TN in spring of 1842. Silas is a resident of Overton Co. and Dicy is a resident of Campbell Co. TN Dicy has intermarried with a James Massengall in Campbell Co. TN 1848.

January Term 1860

Frances J. Goodpasture VS Robert M. Goodpasture bill for divorce he had 3 children by a previous marriage and she possibly had 3 children also by a previous marriage they married about 3 years ago in Kentucky. This is a lengthy divorce of about 9 pages.

Permelia A. Upton VS William Upton petition for divorce married about 9 years ago 5 small children. He was accused of adultery and fornication with Mary Padgett 28, August 1858

8 August 1859 Nathaniel Hollars VS Peggy Jane Hollers bill for divorce married March 1858 in Overton Co. TN. She had repeated acts of adultery and fornication with Joseph Lyons and Alexander Rice and various other persons this was filed 8 August 1859.

September Term 1858

Mary Pharris VS Michael Pharris petition for divorce married about 35 years ago next November Mary resides in Overton Co. TN and Michael resides in Kentucky raised a family of children all grown except they are 2 sons and 1 daughter James M. age 17 years, Jonathan R. age 15 years and Martha age 11 years.

21 March 1858 Alsy Upton VS Wm. E. Upton petition for divorce married about 16 years ago in Overton Co. TN sometime last August Wm left telling Alsey he was going to CA to be gone 5 years he had only gone to Dekalb Co. TN committed acts of adultery and fornication with a woman named Margaret Barnes. Wm. and Alsy had the following children Christopher C. age 13 years and Stephen D. age 7.

Polly A. Flatt VS Ples Flatt petition for divorce married about 4 years ago in Jackson Co. TN lived in Jackson Co. TN lived the last 18 months in Overton Co. TN 3 children Nancy J., Margaret E. and Susanah F. 11 months.

Peter Hooks VS Elizabeth (Perkins) Hooks divorce bill married about 1835 in Blount Co. TN, Elizabeth was accused of adultery with Joseph Stout. October 1849

Ardelia Staggs VS William A. Staggs bill for divorce married 21 December 1843 in Overton Co. TN 2 infant children, October 1849

Record Book 1841 – 1856

Page 7   – 11   Hetty Maxwell VS James Maxwell

Page 251 – 253   George B. Owen VS Lucinda Owen

Page 253 - 255   Charles Crawford VS Emily Crawford

Page 426 - 427   George M. Thompson VS Amy (Looper) Thompson married 1846 Overton Co. TN

Book 1852 - 1857

Page 33-35   Elizabeth Arney VS John Arney

Page 42   John Rains VS Louisa (Richardson) Rains

Page 117-119   Ambrose B. Cope VS Sibby Ann (Mangold) Cope married 1847 Overton Co. TN accused of adultery with S.C. or L. C. Parris of Wayne Co. Kentucky

Page 119-122   John C. Coleman VS Sarah R. (Cox) Coleman married 1840-41 Wayne Co. Kentucky 4 children oldest being Mary E. Coleman age 12, young being Tennessee Coleman age 3.

Page 166-168   Sarah Greer VS John F. Greer married 6 years ago 1846-1847.

Page 169-171   Rebecca Phillips VS Nelson Phillips he is in State Pen in Nashville married 1847 in Campbell Co. TN.

Page 176-177   Elizabeth Shepherd VS George W. Shepherd married 1847 5 children.

Page 211-213   Beda Rayburn VS William Rayburn married 1846 Overton Co. TN.

Page 213-215   Uriah McDonald VS Ann McDonald married 1834 Anderson Co. TN

Page 216-218   Elizabeth Mayfield VS John Mayfield married 184?.

Page 240-242   Sophea Herreford VS Jacob B. Herreford married March 1836 Russell Co. Kentucky.

Page 242–244   Elizabeth (Hargis) Boswell VS Lonzo D. Boswell

Page 244   Thomas Eldridge VS Mahaley Eldridge

Page 263–265   Rebeca Mace VS Wm. Mace married 1846 in Overton Co. TN

Page 311–313   Beda Rayboun VS William Rayboun 1855

Page 313- 317   Nancy Neely VS Thomas J. Neely

Page 393-295   James E. Murray VS Rebecca Jane Murray married 23 February 1852 in Knox Co. TN October 1855

Page 442-445   Nancy (Hall) Grissom VS William Grissom married April 8155 in Overton Co. TN mentions Joseph F. Hall

Page 445–446   Margaret (Smith) Fletcher VS Aaron Fletcher married November 1855 in Overton Co. TN

Page 447-450   Patsy Colston VS William K. or Milton K. Colston married 1848-1849 Overton Co. TN

20 October 1856 Term

Page 19-21   Prudence Bilbrey VS Lawrence Bilbrey

Page 22   Helen Armstrong VS Cullom L. Armstrong

Page 22-25   Sarah Jennings VS Frederick Jennings

Page 25-27   Miles White VS Sara Caroline (Shepherd) White

Page 35-36   Sarah Turner VS William H. Turner

Page 44-46   Susan Carmack VS James Carmack

Page 48-53   Ruth Richardson VS Madison Richardson

Page 56-58   Thomas Eldridge VS Rachel Eldridge

Page 62-64   Thomas P. Wilson VS Joan Wilson

Page 64-65   Celina Belk VS Joseph Belk

Page 117-119   Eliza Rooker VS George Rooker

Page   119-123   Jane McBride VS Thomas McBride

Page   123-124   Ambrose Gore VS Paulina Gore

Page   124-126   Sarah Copeland by friend Henry Gore VS Joseph A. Copeland

Page   126-128   Susan Cargile VS Jacob Cargile

Page   128-129   Joseph Gramer VS Hester Gramer

Page   210-212   Andrew Swallows VS Fanny Swallows

Page   234-235   Polly A. Flatt VS Ples Flatt

Page   238-239   Candis Taylor VS David Taylor

Page   240-243   Alsey Upton VS Wm. E. Upton

Page   243-245   Mary Pharris VS Michael Pharris

Page   320-323   A. J. Newberry VS E. A. Newberry

Page   375-376   Nathaniel Hollers VS Peggy Jane Hollers

Page   380-381   Permelia Upton VS Wm. Upton

Page   382-383   Frances J. Goodpasture VS R. M. Goodpasture

January 1860 Term

Page   396-397   Silas Copeland VS Nancy (Hicks) Copeland married about 1854 in Overton Co. TN

Execution Docket Book 1842-1843

February Term 1842   page 2   The Bank of Tennessee VS Mark
                                    Copeland, James Copeland,
                                    Jefferson Copeland

October Term 1842   Page 75   The heirs and Administrator
                                    of David Stewart deceased VS
                                    Sarah Stewart

February Term 1844   Page 131   Bird Deatherage VS Margaret
                                    Deatherage divorce

February Term 1842   Sarah McDonald VS Thomas
                                    H. McDonald divorce

October Term 1841   Eli Nations VS Milly Nations
                                    petition for divorce

February Term 1841   Page 231   State of Tennessee VS Early
                                    Albertson indictment for
                                    murder also mentions
                                    Solomon Sr.

Court Book 1845 – 1849

Page 6   Samuel A. Hare be appointed
            Administrator of Sally
            Dickson deceased

Miscellaneous Findings

Deed Book B Overton Co. TN Wm. Bunch appointing Solomon
Allred his attorney to sign his name 7 November 1809

Record 1847-1851

State of Tennessee VS Azel Dishman assault and battery October 1845 beat and bruised ill threat on Theapolis Allred

Walker Heirs VS Overton Co. TN page 118 February Docket 1867

February 1852

Murder William Reynolds and Hannah Reynolds charged 27 January 1849 murder of Jeremiah Gray witnesses Green Combs, Nelson Howard, Marah Robbins, Slyvester Robbins, Henry B. Cravins, Richard Lee, Sally Lee, Westley Sells, Henry Nation, Jordan Shoemake, John Smith, Elizabeth Smith, Catherine Cravins not guilty.

April 1868

Ordered by court that G. W. Speck Administrator be allowed further time of 12 months to wind up estate of John Qualls, I. T. Miller, Henry Miller deceased.

MISCELLANEOUS ITEMS

May help to someone with their genealogy research of their family

Microfilm

Page 558-559   5 June 1869   James Robbins died 26 November 1866 in Overton Co. TN give information concerning his death.

Page 562   6 June 1869   State of Tennessee VS Samuel Davis murder 30 January 1869 Davis shot and stabbed Cylen Copeland and Husten Copeland they died instantly, Webster Copeland made affidavit.

Circuit Court Minutes
September 1865 – June 1869

25 September 1865
Malinda Little VS Jacob Little divorce

26 September 1865
Maryan Dodson VS Elbert Dodson divorce

Sarah J. Cullom VS E.N. Cullom and others app. for dower Alvin Cullom Jr. died 1861 500 acres in district 11th on eagle creek had given defendants Louella, Laura H., Sarah E. Tilman Cullom mentioned and named Edward N. Cullom administrator.

28 September 1865
Elizabeth Hardin VS Joseph Hardin divorce

1 October 1859
Obadiah H. Hardin VS Nancy Hardin divorce married

Job Rhom VS Micky Rhom divorce June 1866 married in Overton Co. TN 1858-1859 children are Elizabeth and Martha Ellen, also infant not named

26 September 1866
Mary Daniels VS W. C. Daniels

27 September 1866
Ahi Deck VS Samuel T. Deck attachment

29 September 1866
Parthena Lyon VS Thomas Lyon divorce

State of Tennessee VS Richmond Davis and Catherine Anderson illegal marriage

Isaac T. Ferguson VS Delitha Ferguson divorce married 1861 Jackson Co. TN

Parthena Lyon VS Thomas Lyon divorce decree she was Parthena Bilyue and name was restored to her maiden name 30 January 1867

Elizabeth J. (Wood) Stephens VS Balam L. Stephens divorce decree married 28 June 1863 in Fentress Co. TN he was accused of acts of adultery with one ___________? Miller a woman of ill character

31 January 1867
Margaret Cox VS Enoch Cox divorce

7 February 1867
Eve Wallace VS John Wallace divorce married several years ago in Overton County

1 June 1867
Wm. Richardson VS Nancy ( ) Smith Richardson his app. for dower VS Milton Smith, Louisa Smith, Hardy Smith and Eveline Smith, George A. Smith died in 1864,

7 June 1867
Edward Pryor VS Eliza Pryor petition for divorce

State VS Wm. D. Reed and Gideon Reed murder 27 September 1867 On 1 August 1867 they killed J. T. Poston and he died Solomon Poston prosecutor Nancy Gibbons and Polly Webb were summoned. *Additional note by author J. T. is J. Townsend Poston son of Solomon and Elizabeth (Duke) Poston. He was born about 1840 in Overton Co. TN*

26 September 1867
Brinkley Howard murdered John N. Francis 15 June 1867 killed with an axe

27 September 1867
Dock O. Daulton VS Carrie Daulton divorce decree

27 September 1867
Lafayette L. Smith VS Olea Smith divorce decree

3 October 1867
Mathew Davis Administrator Isaac Davis VS L. W. Oglesby and Amos McBride and James Brown

4 October 1867
State VS Eli Warren and Joseph Pigg murder 1 May 1865 killed George W. Peek and he died instantly James Peek Sr. was the prosecutor

7 October 1869
Jane (Keesling) Chapman VS Samuel M. Chapman

12 October 1867
Patie Breeding VS Biram C. Breeding divorce 4 minor children

25 May 1868
Edward Pryor VS Eliza Pryor divorce

25 May 1868
Eligah Garrett VS Fannie Garrett divorce

25 May 1868
State VS Dock White, Same White and William White

26 May 1868
State VS Martha Mullins bawdy house

4 June 1868
M. J. Reed VS D. B. Reed divorce decree

4 June 1868
Margaret Cox VS Enoch Cox petition for divorce

Eligah Garrett VS Fannie Garrett divorce 28 September 1868 she has been gone for more than 2 years from home

29 September 1868
Rebecca Davis VS Lev. H. Davis petition for divorce

7 October 1868
P. H. Holt VS Jane Holt petition for divorce

16 October 1868
State VS Alexander Tranbarger and Lavergne Buck lewdness

State VS Alexander Tranbarger and Henry Upchurch robbery Henry Upchurch late September 1868 pistol of Carlock Richardson Thomas Sullivan prosecutor

4 June 1869
Ellen A. Carr VS George F. Carr

4 June 1869
Polly A. Ledford VS Delina C. Ledford 275 acres of land conveyed to them by John Smith Sr. in 11th District

7 June 1869
State VS Lee Eldridge prowling on 2 November 1868 in Overton Co.

7 June 1869
State VS Isaac Gore prowling took place on January 1869 he was late of said county

7 June 1869
State VS Thomas Ogletree prowling took place on December 1868 he was late of said county also mention January 1869.

7 June 1869

State VS Baker Bilyue prowling took place on January 1869 he was late of said county it mentioned secret organization known as the Klu Klux Klan

7 June 1869

State VS Marion Carr took place on January 1869 late of said county

7 June 1869

State VS Nick Parker prowling January 1869 late of said county

7 June 1869

State VS A. J. Danner prowling December 1868 and January 1869 late of said county

7 June 1869

State VS Creed Mainord prowling December 1868 and January 1869 late of said county

7 June 1869

State VS Marion Danner prowling December 1868 late of said county

7 June 1869

State VS Joseph Parker prowling January 1869 late of said county

7 June 1869

State VS Lindsey Turner prowling January 1869 late of said county

7 June 1869

State VS Joseph Davis prowling January 1869 late of said county

7 June 1869

State VS John Johnson prowling January 1869 late of said county

Miscellaneous court findings of interest

16 December 1876

page 596 Mary E. Huddleston VS Martin V. Huddleston Decree mentions children Bethialine Huddleston age about 6 years to be committed to defendant and that the custody of Sarah Bice and Creed Taylor Huddleston the other issue of said marriage be committed to the complainant and that defendant pay all cost.

Page 597

P. Brown VS Alvan Brown divorce

10 April 1877

page 623 W. H. Smith VS Sarah Smith divorce came the plantiff by attorney and dismisses his suit and assumes cost

11 April 1877

page 632
A. W. Smith VS Nancy V. Smith divorce

Front Beaty and Ina (Peterman) Ledbetter with children Roy, Rocky, Quitman and Hazel.

Laken Beaty Ledbetter born 10 March 1863 Overton Co. TN died 27 August 1937 married 4 January 1890 Overton Co. TN to Ina Peterman born 7 June 1874 died 27 August 1956 son Roy born about 1916 died 13 September 1984, Rockey born 2 July 1910 died 17 September 1932, Quitman born 17 July 1905 died 15 April 1960, Hazel born 25 September 1907 died 17 March 1986 they were more children in this family.

Beaty and Ina along with several children of this family are buried at the Hoover Cemetery in Allons community in Overton County TN. Beaty was the son of Eljah Washington Ledbetter and Annalisa (Garrett) Ledbetter which raised a large family and has many descendants living in Overton County today. Ina (Peterman) Ledbetter was the daughter of Sib Riley Peterman and wife Serena J. (Hunter) Peterman they also raised a large family.

Thomas J. and Elzada J. (White) Garrett

Thomas J. Garrett born 25 December 1846 died 15 August 1920 married 20 May 1877 Overton County TN to Elzada J. White born 4 August 1854 died 11 January 1918 both are buried in the T. J. Daniels cemetery in Overton County. Thomas J. was the son of David and Catherine Garrett and Elzada was the daughter of John Dillard White and Mary (McMillan) White.

Thomas and Elzada raised 11 children known they are William Columbus "Bill", Joe Miller, Joel Sparks, Mary Catherine married a Whited, John L., Rebecca married Terry Norris, Nancy E., Robert Thurston, James Harris, Ibba, Millard Filmore.

Census information on this family
1880 Census Overton Co. TN Dist.#11/225-225
Thomas J. Garrott 33 m TN; Elzada J. 24 f TN; Joe M. 2 m son TN; Joel S. 4/12 Feb. m son TN; William C. Whyte7 m step-son TN.

Made about 1912 at the Dale/Spicer Cemetery in Overton County TN near the Clay County line going from Hilham area.

1900 Census Overton Co TN Dist#11/217-217

Thomas J. Garrett 56 m Dec. 1843 m/23yrs TN VA TN farmer, Elzadie 47 f Aug 1852 12children/11living TN TN TN, Joe Miller 22 m Dec 1877 TN, Joel Sparks 20 m Feb 1880 TN, Mary C. 18 f Feb 1882 TN, John L. 16 m Feb 1884 TN, Rebecca J. 14 f Mch 1886 TN, Nancy E. 11 f Aug 1888 TN, Robert Thurston 9 m Feb 1891 TN, James Harris 5 m Aug 1894 TN, Ibba 4 f Jan 1896 TN, Millard F. 2 m Jan 1898 TN.

1910 Census Overton Co TN Dist#11/34-34

Thomas J Garrett 63 m TN VA TN m/35yrs farmer, Elzadie 55 f TN TN TN 12children/11living, Joel S Garrett 30 m son TN, Nancy E. 20 f dau. TN, Thurston 18 m son TN, James H. 16 m son TN, Ibby 13 f dau. TN, Millard 11 m son TN, Alvin 22mths/12 m gson TN.

1920 Census Overton Co TN Dist#11/215-215

Thomas J Garrett 75 m wd TN own/farm, Nancy E. 29 f dau TN, Robert 28 m son TN, James H 25 m son TN, Millard F 22 m son TN, Myrtle 20 f dau/law TN, Hoy H 6 m gdson TN, Robert H 4 m gdson TN, Auda D 11mths f gddau TN.

Those is in the picture that can be identified are back row L-R Barney, Nathan, James Anderson "Ance", Alice, Hobson, Luther, Raleigh, front row L-R unknown, Beatrice, Marvin Wilson, Simmie . If someone can identify the other ones in the picture or correct mistaken ones that are identified please contact author.

Obituary for James Anderson "Ance" Dale
January 3, 1936

Injuries Received in fall from barn causes death of man; Funeral services fro Ance J. Dale, 76, a farmer of the Sixth District of Overton County, who died at his home in north Livingston, on Tuesday, Dec. 31, at 4:00 a.m. of injuries received when he fell from his loft some ten days ago were conducted on Wednesday afternoon at 1 o'clock, by the Rev. James T. Hooten at Cedar Hill, with burial in the Spicer cemetery. He had been twice married, first to Miss Martha Lynn, who died thirthy years ago. His second wife, Mrs. Loucetta Overton Dale, survives. He is also survived by four sons, Barney, Hobson B., Luther and Maryvin Dale, all of Overton County.

Early Court Records Overton Co. TN
extracts from the case filed

1848
B. C. Sewell Administrator VS John Kennedy and others petition to sell land

Patrick Pool deceased died 26 March 1848 Overton County TN, B. C. Sewell administrator Nancy Jane, Mary, Winiford, Martha E. Sarah Hannah, and heirs at law of Decauter Patrick, Robert H. and Patrick M. Pool of Desert County Illinois, James V. Pool residence unknown Sarah C. and Mary E. Pool, Winniford who intermarried with John Kennedy, Martha J. Pook who intermarried with petitioner all of Overton County TN are all heirs at law of Patrick Pool deceased. Sarah. Patrick V. and Mary E. heirs of Robert Pool deceased are minors under 21 John Kennedy is guardian of Mary E. and Patrick V. Patrick V., M. Decauter Patrick, Nancy Jane, Mary, Winniford Martha E. and Sarah, Hannah Pool all minors under 21 and have no regular guardian, John Kennedy being appointed guardian.

1849

Evan Bartlett VS Champlain Langford petition

Evan Bartlett administrator of John R. Jones deceased in Overton County TN against Champlain Langford and Nancy his wife, Watsdale Kendle and Susan his wife, James Clark and Jane his wife, Fanny Jones, David Jones, Betsy Jones, Pheby Jones, Mary Jones, Martha Jones the later minors of their guardian Robert Peak. John R. Jones died 19, January 1849 in Overton County TN died with no wife of children the above are brothers and sisters only heirs of Edward Jones.

1848

Ruth A. Huddleston, Bethiah L. ? VS Heirs of C. T. Huddleston petition for dower

Creede T. Huddleston died 1847 in Mexico his children Martha V., Simon W., Ruth A., Louiza C., all are minors and have no regular guardian

1848

John H. Chapin administrator and Others VS Exparte petition to sell land

John H. Chapin administrator of Paul Chapin deceased died in 1847 Hiram Chapin, George More and his wife Mary, Harrison Chapin, John Chapin, Josiah Chapin, Silas Chapin, Franklin Chapin, Alsey Chapin, Catherine Chapin the latter six by guardian John H. Chapin on legal heirs and representatives of John H. Chapin deceased. Paul Chapin died 9 November 1847 in Overton County TN leaving John H., Hiram, Paul, Jacob Garrett and Polly his wife, Harrison, John, Josiah, Silas, Franklin, Alzy, Catherine.

1848

Elizabeth Hinds and Others VS Exparte petition to sell land

Elizabeth Hinds, Nancy Weaver, Josiah Hinds, Claiborn Hinds, John Hinds, Clinton Hinds, Sterling Harris and Wife Mary, Davis Masters and wife Sussannah, Samuel Loftis and wife Elizabeth, Thomas S. Anderson and Sarah Anderson, William Pharris and wife Caroline, Simeon Hinds Jr., Elizabeth widow of Simeon Hinds Sr. died 1840 Overton County TN and others are the only heirs at law of deceased.

1848 June Term

John S. Copeland Heirs

George W. Copeland, Sarah G. wife of Lewis Bilbrey, Nancy C. Copeland, Josiah R. Copeland, Eliza L. Copeland, John S. Copeland the last four being minors and their guardian is George W. Copeland. All the above are heirs of John S. Copeland who died in 1842 in Overton County TN. Petitioners are also the only heirs of deceased grandfather Josiah Copeland who also died in Overton County TN.

1848 February

Heirs of Edward Jones VS Exparte petition

Jane wife of James Clark, Susan wife of __________ Kendle, John Jones, Francis Davis, Elizabeth, Pheba, Polly, Martha Jones the four being under age 21 years of age by their guardian Robert Peak. All heirs of deceased Edward Jones died in 1844 Overton County TN, also mentioned are the following Nancy Jones, Fanny Jones, Polly Jones, Davis Jones, John Jones, Betsy Jones, Jane E. Clark.

1848 October

James R. Copeland etal. VS Exparte petition to sell land

Martha Copeland wife of Thomas Gardenhire, William B.

Copeland, John L. Copeland, Thompson G. Copeland, Martin V. Copeland the last three by guardian James R. Copeland all heirs of Stephen C. Copeland deceased in Mexico in 1847.

Explanation of the miscellaneous records

From the author: the reason I have included so many of the divorce extracts and other miscellaneous court extracts is after collecting and researching genealogy records from so many different sources. You never know what you will find. Also it has been mislead that all records with the exception of our deed records were destroyed in the courthouse fire in 1865. That is not true, although there was a fire and several record books from other offices in the county survived and are on microfilm. They are not indexed sometimes, but are very valuable, and as any researchers know, you just have to read them page per page. I have shared so many of these findings with people who have contacted me on their family. I thought it would be good to include some in the genealogy section of this book. It will be worthwhile if it helps just one person further their hunt for an ancestor.

I have several complete files on some of these extracts as well if someone is interested and wants to contact me. On any one extract I have included. If I have the complete file record, I will be glad to share it. If I don't have the file, I can tell you where to locate it whether on microfilm or loose file.

Our Overton County Archives houses many of the original books and loose records also that survived this fire. The archive is a real asset to research Overton County ancestry.

Laura Belle, Horace and Willie

Children of Franklin Hammock who died at the skirmish or battle of Raven Cliff in Overton County in 1864 this was between Tinker Dave Beaty group and the Hammock gang organized by Franklin

Laura Belle (Hammock) born 14 February 1860 Overton County TN died 13 February 1936 Macon County TN buried in the Pleasant Valley cemetery she married Sam Omega Murphy they had 3 children Joseph, Lula and Zula.

Horace Hammock born

Thomas Horace Hammock born 11 August 1863 Overton County TN died 7 November 1940 Morgan County TN he married 1st to Juliet (Crabtree) they possibly had two children then he married 25 August 1885 Overton County TN to Sara Elizabeth (Harris) they had seven children. Thomas Horace and Sarah Elizabeth are both buried at the Durham Cemetery in Fentress County TN.

Hannah Martelia (Claborn) Nation with sons left Arlie Quitman
Nation and Haskell Elvin Nation made about 1940-1942 in
Oklahoma

Hannah Martelia (Claborn) was born 23 January 1874 in Overton
County TN died 12 December 1962 in Caddo County Oklahoma
buried in the Memory Lane Cemetery in Oklahoma she was the
daughter of John Tanner Claborn and Mary Jane (Tranbarger)
Claborn. Martelia married Henry Jackson Nation 19 July 1894 in
Overton County TN.

Haywood Tanner Claborn and Martelia (Claborn) Nation
brother and sister taken about 1960 in Oklahoma

Andrew J. White and Nancy Jane (Swafford) White
Andrew J. White was born 4 August 1875 died 22 April 1965
married Nancy Jane (Swafford) she was born 25 January 1886
died 20 April 1957 they both are buried in the Liberty Cemetery
in Overton County TN

Mary Ann oldest, Dimple and Thomas Herbert Swafford

Children of Charlie and Milda (Walker) Swafford and grandchildren of Louis Swafford, Mary Ann (Swafford) born 16 May 1910 died2 October 1997 married Robert Herman McDonald both are buried in Liberty Cemetery in Overton County TN also is Thomas Herbert born in 10 October 1915 died 25 June 1992

Lillie Mae (Swafford) McCormick

She was born April 1893 died 5 February 1945 buried at
Bethlehem Cemetery in Overton County TN married Shirley A.
McCormick they raised 6 children one was Norine (McCormick)
who was born about 1912 and then Opal about 1916 another
daughter was Ola born about 1918 there were some others also.
Shirley was on the 1920 Census in Overton County with these
first three daughters.

Norine McCormick the baby she is holding could be her sister Opal who was born about 1916, since this picture was labeled Norine McCormick

Andrew Virgil Ledbetter and (Collins) Ledbetter and three of their youngest children Andrew was born 12 June 1875 died 20 January 1950 married 9 August 1896 in Overton County to Minnie (West) born 17 November 1878 died 5 May 1964 they both are buried in the Bethlehem cemetery.

Aquilla (Collins) Ledbetter with Onie and Hershel

Aquilla was mother of Andew Virgil Ledbetter and other children she was born 13 July 1854 died 15 March 191 7 buried at J. C. Ledbetter cemetery in Overton County TN.

Ledbetter Brothers Andrew Virgil, James Overton, William Porter. These are 3 sons of James C. and Aquilla (Collins) Ledbetter

Oliver Ledbetter born 4 February 1891 died 6 May 1919 buried in J. C. Ledbetter Cemetery he was son of James C. and Aquilla (Collins) Ledbetter he was a brother to the above three Ledbetter brothers.

Reuben Walker

He was born between 1790-1796 in NC died 18 April 1876 in Overton County TN buried in the Allred Cemetery, was married twice having children by both spouses for a total of about 13 children many descendants still live in the Overton, Clay, Putnam County and areas close by today.

Rufus Mitchell "Piker" Dishman

He was grandson of Reuben Walker, Rebecca Walker daughter of
Reuben and Aggy (Copeland) Walker was married 21 July 1872
in Overton County to John Henry Dishman they are the parents
of several children "Piker" is the great grand grandfather of the
author Ronald Dishman.

David Leander Jr. & Sarah Amanda "Mandy" (Stover) Sells

David L. Sells was born 12 October 1835 died 14 May 1908 married 1 February 1866 in Overton County TN to Sarah Amanda "Mandy" (Stover) she was born 11 December 1848 died 26 October 1922 both are buried in the Sells Cemetery in Overton County. They raised 9 children all living to adulthood and marrying except for one daughter.

Jessie Stover and Sister Sarah Amanda (Stover) Sells

Jessie and Sarah Amanda were children of Hiram and Minerva (Phillips) Stover they had 7 other children besides the two in the photograph above. Jesse W. was born 26 October 1844 died 18 March 1925 buried in Jesse Stover cemetery in Overton County. He was in the Co. B 4th TN Cav. C.S.A.

Rebecca (Sells) Holman with 3 daughters Nova, Audra, Estie

Rebecca (Sells) Holman born 30 October 1870 died 23 July 1967 buried Sells cemetery daughter of David L. and Sarah Amanda (Stover) Sells she married 3 October 1892 to Andrew Holman they raised 2 sons besides the 3 daughters in picture above the sons were David Grant and Edward Floyd.

Andrew and Rebecca Holman with 2 youngest children Grant oldest and Andrew is holding Nova she was born 30 June 1896 and Grant was born 26 August 1893 then next child Floyd was born in December 1898 so this was made between 1896 1898.

Rebecca (Sells) Holman sitting in front, children in back are Audra, Floyd, Nova, Grant and Estie.

Andrew Holman

He was born 1 January 1863 died 29 December 1902 son of Rubin and Minerva (Tayes) Holman he had 7 siblings. Andrew died when just 39 years old and left his wife Rebecca to raise their 5 children which was very hard time then she did a good job raising the children by herself they work the farm and raised crops and other things that were needed at that time period. Grant the oldest child made and preacher and the youngest child Audra made a teacher.

Mrs. Ollie Robbins shown making a rug 19 February 1946

Mrs. Ollie (Smith) born 26 June 1894 died 23 July 1961 married Sam Allen Robbins born 29 June 1885 died 15 April 1963 both are buried at Greenhill Cemetery in Overton County TN

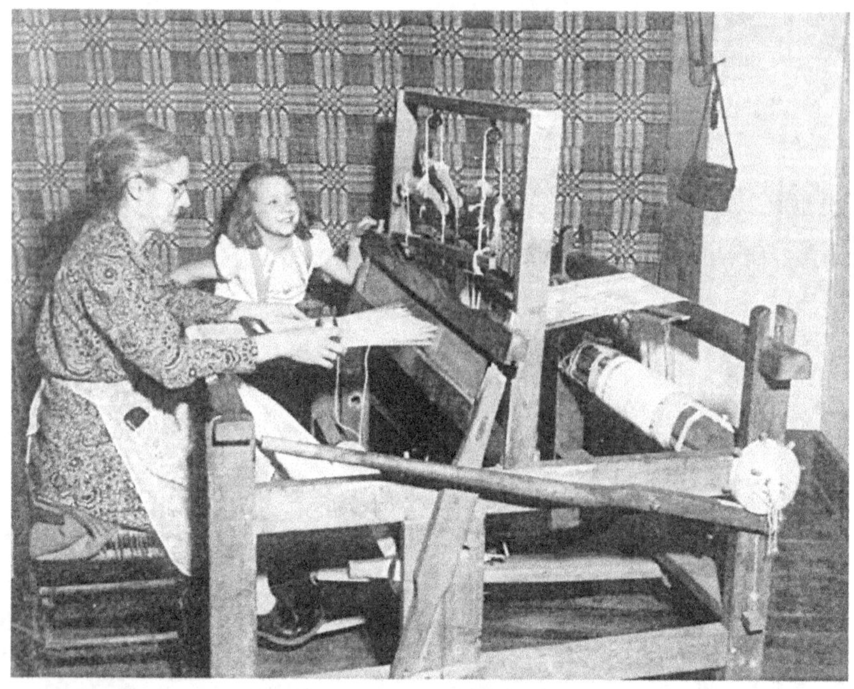

Mrs. Ollie Robbins shown using a large old fashioned loom 19 February 1946. She lived in the Alpine area of Overton County TN.

Arizona (Franklin) Sells weaving on a large loom. She lived in the Alpine area of Overton County. She was born 9 October 1897 died 15 December 1986. She was daughter of David and Elmira Franklin, married Nasby Sells. He was born 5 May 1892 died 4 March 1935. Both are buried at the Falling Springs Cemetery in Overton County TN.

Doctor Walter F. Sidwell born 11 February 18 75 died 12 January 1953, married on 28 March 1899 to Ada Ann (Arms). She was born 23 December 1877 died 29 November 1962 Both are buried at Good Hope Cemetery in Overton Co. TN

Bledsoe Family

Front row C___ Upchurch, Laura (Bledsoe) Upchurch, Margaret Bledsoe. Back row Jesse Bledsoe, William "Bill" Bledsoe, Charles Bledsoe

Margaret (Neely) Bledsoe born 11 October 1847 KY died 2 December 1924 buried in Bledsoe Cemetery in Livingston Overton County, she was the widow of Charles Tribune Bledsoe born 20 March 1838 died 18 December 1878 Overton County. He was a Private in Co. F 8th TN Infantry in the C.S.A. buried at the Bledsoe Cemetery. Laura A. (Bledsoe)

Upchurch, daughter of Margaret and Charles Tribune Bledsoe. The young Upchurch is a grandson living with Margaret his grandmother and Uncles Jesse and Charles on the 1900 census in Livingston Overton County. Charles was born 1 September 1875 died 30 January 1975 in San Antonia TX and is buried there. Jesse A. Bledsoe born 16 April 1878 died 31 May 1961 in Tarrant

County Texas buried in Mansfield Cemetery. William "Bill" Bledsoe2 March 1873 died 17 January 1933, buried in the Bledsoe Cemetery in Livingston also. Laura was thought to have died in Florida.

Bledsoe Cemetery

This family cemetery is very unique because of the fact that a complete solid concrete wall surrounds it with no gate to access it at all…you have to actually clime over wall to get to the cemetery. To see pictures of this and read a story of this cemetery, go to www. josephinesjournal.com It is listed as Bledsoe Cemetery story.

Emmitt Cecil & Mary E. "Myrtie" (Stover) Claborn with granddaughter

Emmitt Cecil Claborn born 30 Decem 1902 died May 1975 in Shawnee Oklahoma married Mary E. "Myrtie" (Stover) she was born 3 March 1900 died March 1975 in Oklahoma also they are both buried in Oklahoma she was the daughter James W. Stover and Arnetie (Hammock) Stove. Emmitt was the son of James R. "Jimmy" Claborn and Liza (Reagan) Claborn. Both have many relatives still living in Overton County today as they came from a large family.

Lonnie Claborn son of Cecil Claborn and Myrtie (Stover) Claborn

The author met Lonnie for the first time in the 1980's in Oklahoma on a genealogy trip this was made in Oklahoma when the author first met him.

Joseph Ewing Nation and wife Donnie (Smith) Nation with children: L-R Gusta, Ressie, Marie, Irene

Joseph Ewing Nation born 4 June 1895 died 15 August 1975 married 16 May 1918 to Donnie (Smith) born 18 July 1897 died 20 January 1988 both are buried at Crestlawn Cemetery in Putnam County TN. J. Ewing was son of John Wesley and Anna Belle (Robbins) Nation and Donnie was daughter of John Oscar Smith and Nancy Haggard (Means) Smith.

Talton B. Maynard and Ida (Nation) Maynard with
children Jewell, Pearl, Wesley Buford

Talton B. Maynard was son of Robert D. and Mary (Marcom) Maynard Ida (Nation) was a sister to Joseph Ewing in the picture above. Talton and Ida both are buried in the Crestlawn Cemetery in Putnam County.

Lacy and Laura (Claborn) Adkins with Willie Fletcher
as young boy

Lacy Adkins born30 April 1898 died 5 January 1979 married
Laura E. (Claborn) born 17 February 1906 died 6 September 1989
both are buried in the Fellowship Cemetery in Overton County.
Lacy was son of John and Louella (Flowers) Adkins and Laura
was daughter of Jimmy and Liza (Reagan) Claborn.

James R "Jimmy" and Liza (Reagan) Claborn

James R Claborn born 16 October 1872 died 10 December 1957 married 3 May 1894 Overton County to Liza (Reagan) born 4 June 1875 died 10 October 1955. Both are buried at Sells Cemetery in Overton County TN.

Johnnie Mike Nation made Oklahoma. Notice the bed inside the screened in area in front yard at his home. I assume they slept outside in this or would take naps during the day outside. Johnnie was born 23 April 1903 Overton County TN died 22 March 2000 at 96 years young buried at Memory Lane Cemetery, Anadarko Oklahoma. He was son of Henry Jackson Nation and Hannah Martelia (Claborn) Nation. Moved to Oklahoma when young, married and raised his family there.

L-R John, Tom, and Jim Zachary brothers

John A. Logan born 15 August 1885 died 1 November 1961, Thomas Grant born 19 May 1883 died 31 March 1966, James Alexander born 19 September 1872 died 8 April 1945, all three are sons of Pleasant Jasper Zachacy and Margaret (Tranbarger) Zachary.

July 1994 Tranbarger Reunion TN

Addie, Edna and Mabel Tranbarger sisters at the grave of their grandfather James Tranbarger buried in the Sells Cemetery in Overton County TN.

Addie M. (Tranbarger) born 20 December 1908 died 28 January 2002 Howell Co Missouri, Edna E. (Tranbarger) Covey born 13 December 1906, Beulah Mable (Tranbarger) Rogers born 31 July 1910 they are daughters of John Boles Tranbarger and Louella (Garrett) Tranbarger who left Overton County in the 1890's and raised their family in Missouri.

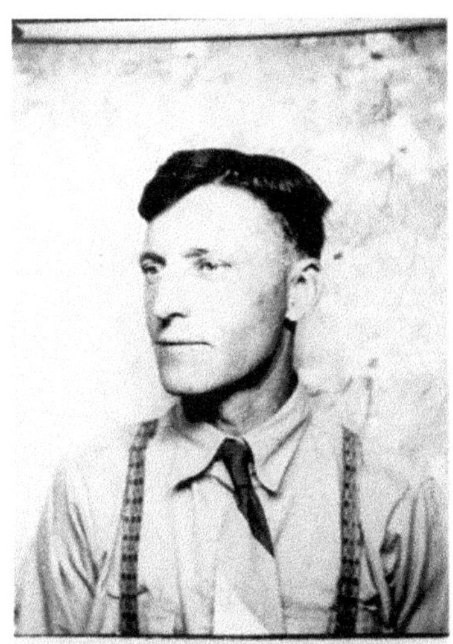

Theodore Jackson Tranbarger

Made 16 June 1941 in Mountain View MO he was son of John Boles Tranbarger and Louella (Garrett) Tranbager born 8 August 1899 died October 1981 Independence Montgomery Co KS.

Jesse Alexander Tranbarger Horse Trainer

Jesse Alexander Tranbarger born 12 April 1887 died 7 September 1965 Oklahoma he was son of William Alexander Tranbarger and Mary Emily (Poor) Tranbarger who were both born in TN.

Jesse Alexander Tranbarger made 26 October 1926 in
Ponco City Oklahoma

L-R Charles W., Nannie, Annis, Ida and
Catherine N. "Kittie" (Cox) Sells Children of "Kittie"

Catherine (Cox) Sells born 1886 Overton Co TN died 1935 in
Florida daughter of Charlie Cox and Nancy (Stover) Cox. Many
relatives still reside in Overton County today.

Robert Lee "Bob" and Ova (Huffer) Sells with children
Bonnie, Barnie, Nancy Ellen, Andrew, Forest, Halton

Robert Lee Sells born 18 April 1886 died 20 June 1956 married
Ova Leatha (Huffer) she was born 15 July 1889 died 14 January
1981 both of them are buried at Sells & Stover Overton County
TN.

Malissa (Myers) Cullom & Wheeler "Rub" Cullom

Malissa (Myers) was born 20 January 1903 died 23 February 1991 daughter of Jerry Myers and Amanda (Wilson) Myers. She married Willis Wheeler "Rube" Cullom born 20 Sep 1908 died 20 August 1993 son of Rubin Cullom and Dora Frances (Hill) Cullom. Rube and Malissa both are buried at Bethlehem Cemetery in Overton County near other relatives.

Robert Sidney Myers and Caroline L. (Cullom) Myers with
small child

Robert Sidney was born 16 August 1895 died 23 March 1972
married Caroline L. (Cullom) born 21 May 1907 died 16 February
1990 both are buried at Bethlehem Cemetery in Overton Co TN.
Sidney is a brother to Malissa (previous page) and Caroline is a
sister to Rube in the story and picture prior.

Leslie Aaron Keeton

Leslie Aaron Keeton born about 1907 died 7 October 1980 married Allie Mae (Cullom) about 1911 died 15 September 1983. Both are buried at Bethlehem Cemetery in Overton County.

Leslie Keeton when a young man worked as a cook along side of his mother at the Old Maynord Hotel that was in Livingston on the 1920 Census for Overton County he and his mother were both listed as Hotel Cooks the proprietor of the Hotel was a Maynord. After he left the Hotel he went to work at Ideal Laundry in

Livingston and this is were he worked until having to give up work Willard Maynord owned the Laundry.

Leslie and Allie Mai raised their children in home where the current Livingston bypass is today when they were going to build the bypass they had to move so Leslie and Allie Mai bough the Old Longview Scholl building in 1970 which was the Colored school before its closing and they remodeled and made this into their home. They lived here the remainder of their lives. John Keeton their son still lives in the house today. Their son John Keeton still lives in this home today located on Spring Street in Livingston.

Rebecca Keeton

She was born December 1883 died 4 December 1964 buried in the Cash Cemetery in Livingston Overton County TN.

1920 Census Overton Co. TN
She is living in the household of her parents and this is listed with her parents documentation.

1930 Census Overton Co. TN Dist.#6/112
Rebecca and her son Leslie are listed with the James. L. Maynard who is listed as Hotel proprieter in the Town of Livingston. Listed as below.

Rebecca Keeton 42 f n TN TN TN Hotel Cook read/write no
Lesle Keeton 22 m n TN TN TN Hotel Cook read/write yes

Obituary 10 December 1964
Rebecca Keeton Buried in Cash Cemetery: Funeral services for Mrs. Rebecca Keeton of Route 1 Cookeville were conducted Sunday December 6, at 2:00 p.m. from McDonald Zion Baptist Church. Reverend Leroy Jackson was the officiating minister. Interrment was in Cash Cemetery with Speck-Hyder Funeral Home in charge of arrangements. Mrs. Keeton died at her home on Friday December 4. She was 78 years of age. She was born in Livingston in 1884 and was the daughter of Tom and Liza Keeton. She was a Methodist. Survivors include a son, Leslie A. Keeton; five grandchildren and two great grandchildren.

Rebecca worked for many private families in their home around Livingston along with working at the Maynord Hotel untill it closed.

Irene (Cullom) Bohannon & Rube Cullom
Allie Mae (Cullom) Keeton sisters with their brother. There were
4 girls and 1 boy. Their parents were Rubin Cullom and Dora
Frances (Hill) Cullom.

Allie Mae (Cullom) Keeton & Rub Cullom
Sister & Brother children of Rubin Cullom and Dora Frances
(Hill) Cullom

Miscellaneous information on Cullom Family
1910 Census Overton Co. TN Dist.#6/68-71

Rubin Cullom 24 m b Hd m1 7yrs TN TN TN R general farm; Dora F. 27 A mu wife m1 7yrs 2-2 TN TN TN; Caroline E. 3 f mu dau. TN TN TN; Willis W. 1 9/12 m mu son TN TN TN; Caroline Hill 57 f mu wd 3-3 mother in law TN TN TN; Minerva J. Hill unknown f b wd grandmother in law TN US US.

1920 Census Overton Co. TN Dist.#6/ward 3/63-65

Reuben Cullom 37 m b md TN rent Hd; Dora 33 f b md TN wife; Caroline 13 f b dau. TN; Willie W. 11 m b son TN; Alla May 9 f b dau. TN; Hattie Ann 5 f b dau. TN; Irene 3 f b dau. TN.

1930 Census Overton Co. TN

Dora and her children are living in the household of her mother Carolyn she is listed as widow with 4 children living in the household. This is listed in documentation under her mother Carolyn.

1870 Census Fentress Co TN Dist#3/1-1

Caroline Hill was listed as domestic servant living in the household of Alexander and Charity Copeland who are her sister and brother in law most likely also living in the household is Jackson Hill 12 years old male. Have a copy of this record.

Also note that Manerva Hill who is probably the mother of Charity, Caroline, Jackson is living with this same Alexander Copeland on the 1880 census in Fentress County and listed as mother in law.

1870 Census Fentress Co TN

Caroline Hill 18 f, Jackson 12 m, Minerva 56 f all living in the household of Alexander Copeland son in law of Minerva and brother in law of Caroline so Charity was a sister to Caroline and daughter of Minerva.

1880 Census Overton Co TN Dist.#11
Caroline Hill Sidney Hill Dora F Hill living in the household of
Benjamin Carlock

1900 Census Overton Co. TN Dist.#11
Caroline Hill 46 f Apr. 1854 wd 3/3 Hd; Dora F. 17 f Nov. 1882
dau.;James. B. 15 m Sep. 1884 son; Manerva J. 77 1823 wd 3/3
have a copy of this record.

1910 Census Overton Co. TN Dist.#6
She is living in the household of her son in law Rubin Cullom
and this is in documentation in his notes.

1920 Census

1930 Census Overton Co. TN Dist.#6
Carolyne Hill 80 f n wd 24 TN TN TN; Dora F. Cullom 46 f n 19
wd TN TN TN laundress; W. Wheeler 21 m n son TN TN TN
truck driver; Allie M. 20 f n dau. TN TN TN; Hettie A. 17 f n dau.
TN TN TN; Irene 15 f n dau. TN TN TN.

Have a copy of her death record it list her parents as Jordan
Hill born in TN and Jane Hill born in TN Dora Cullom was the
informant burial was listed as Eagle Creek her occupation was
listed as Cook.

Caroline L. (Cullom) Myers & Ida E. (Roberts) Springs

Ida E. (Roberts) Springs born March 1887 died 6 July 1979 buried Cash Cemetery in Livingston Overton County TN. She was a descendant of the Roberts Family Slaves in the Alpine are of Overton County. Herself and her daughters Mabel and Alice were highly respected in the Livingston area. The Author even knew Ida and cherishes the times he spent with her and wishes that he had inquired more from her about her history and the history of the county while visiting years ago. Her daughters Mabel and Alice shared much information and helped the author in early years of collecting history for the county.

Original postcard photograph of Aunt Liz Allred with Rose Hart Dale age 2 this was made about 1912 in Livingston at the Dale home in the backyard feeding chickens. This photo is of the location where First Christian Church now stands. The author is the proud owner of this postcard and it has never been postmark.

Obituary 8 May 1918

"Aunt" Liz Allred, a faithful old colored "mammy" whose early life dated back to the Civil War, died Sunday morning after a short illness. She stepped on a nail about a week ago which resulted in blood poison that caused her death. "Aunt" Liz who remembered and related many of the hardships suffered by the South during the war, was one of the few surviving slaves, and possibly the oldest in this section. She did not know her exact age, but she was probably about eighty at the time of her death. The remains of "Aunt" Liz were buried Monday morning in the Cash graveyard.

For more information on this and other great stories you can go to Josephine's Journal website. www.josephinesjournal.com

Joe Claude Bohannon, Sidney Myers and
Wheeler "Rube" Cullom

Joe Claude Bohannon born 18 June 1908 died 9 April 1994 he married Irene (Cullom) sister to Rube Cullom he was married to a sister of Sidney Myers. So they were brother in law in perspective I guess you would say.

Jerry Myers and Amanda (Wilson) Myers raised a large family
in Overton County

1900 Census Overton Co. TN Dist.#2.
Jerry Myers 32 m Jun. 1867 Hd. m15; Martha M. E. 26 f Dec. 1873 wf 6-5; Sarah A. 9 f Nov. 1890 dau.; James A. 6 m Jly 1893 son; Robert S. 4 m Aug. 1895 son; Miria A. 2 f Sep. 1897 dau.; Samuel C. 10/12 m Jly 1899 son.

1910 Census Overton Co. TN Dist.#33-33

Jerry Myers 46 m b m1 26yrs Hd TN TN TN farmer; Manda M. 36 f b m1 12/7 TN TNTN; Sallie M. 18 f b dau. TN TN TN; Early 15 m b son TN TN TN; Robert C. 13 m b son TN TN TN; Minnie 7 f b dau. TN TN TN; Mary M. 6 f b dau. TN TN TN; Ella M. 5 f b TN TN TN; Daisy D. 10/12 f b dau. TN TN TN.

Obituary 31 May 1935

Jerry Myers, Colored 67 Dies Saturday
Jerry Myers 67 highly respected and widely known negro of Overton county died Saturday after an illness of several months. He was a son of the late Bush Myers, who was a slave of Capt. Calvin E. Myers, before the Civil War. He is survived by his second wife, Mrs. Belle Myers, two sons Sid and Charlie Myers, three daughters Mrs. Myra Anderson of Celina, Mrs. Minnie Copeland and Miss Lissie Myers, and one sister Mrs. Myra Maynord. Funeral services werre held Sunday with burial in the Wilson cemetery on Roaring River.

Have a copy of his death records it has a lot of information in it.

Clarence, Clester, Carlis Cravens all were brothers

Cravens Brothers name they went by all began with letter C although they had other names as well. The Boys names began with letter C and the girls with letter E and they also had other names although they used the E names. They were the children of Albert Laken Cravens and Tilda Ann (Claborn) Cravens.

Albert J. "Clarence" Cravens was born 17 February 1901 died 22 January 1962 buried at Goodhope Cemetery in Livingston, John Henry "Clester" Cravens was born 5 August 1904 died 9 March 1959 buried at Howard's Chapel/Daniels Cemetery on the Twin Oaks Road in Overton County TN, Bennie "Carlis" Haywood Cravens born 20 February 1913 died 10 January 1974 buried at Goodhope Cemetery in Livingston.

The girls names were "Ellen" Jane (Cravens) Ogletree, "Effie" Rosan (Cravens) Perkins, Mary "Ethel" (Cravens) Dishman the authors grandmother, "Easter" Leona (Cravens) Ledbetter.

Mary "Ethel" (Cravens) Dishman

She is walking down broad street about where the community center is located at present time.

Alvin Haiston Ramsey born 2 April 1847 died 5 September 1905 married 17 Nove 1878 to Candis (Cantrell) born 11 January 1860 died 22 March 1928 they both are buried at the Deck Cemetery in Overton County.

James M "Jim" Copeland born 29 March 1883 died15 November 1936 married about 1908 to Mindie L (Ramsey) born 31 January 1890 died 13 May 1958 both are buried in Liberty Cemetery in Overton County. The little boy Jim is holding is suppose to be Herman their first born child.

Oren Vaughn born 14 March 1889 died 26 November 1972 married 1 April 1906 to Lucy E. (Ramsey) born 26 September 1886 died 13 August 1965 they both are buried in the Taylor Place Cemetery in Fentress County Tennessee. Children in the photograph are Maude Lee (Vaughn) born 18 April 1909 died 21 October 1975 married Carver Poston buried at Zions Hill Cemetery in Overton County, Mae Vaughn born 30 March 1911 died 12 Decemeber 1989 buried at Memorial Gardens Cemetery in Overton County, Boyd Ervin Vaughn born 16 March 1913 died 25 November 1986 buried Memorial Gardens Cemetery Overton County married Edith (Copeland), other child is suppose to be Roy Vaughn

Robert Lee Vaughn born 27 January 1873 died 17 October 1940 married 5 January 1893 in Overton County to Millie Jane (White) born 4 August 1871 died 17 October 1935 both are buried in the Liberty Cemetery in Overton County. They raised 11 children all of their children's names boys and girls started with the letter C.

The children are Cordia Ann born 24 October 1894 died 29 January 1980 married 10 March 1912 to Thomas Millard Oakley born 11 February 1890 died 25 July 1977 both are buried at Goodhope Cemetery in Overton County, Cortes Vaughn, Corbit Vaughn born 19 September 1896 died 12 January buried at Liberty Cemetery, Connie Vaughn married Pete Farley, Clydia Lee born 6 June 1900 died 10 February 1998 married 11 November 1921 to C. Clay Parsons Sr. born 29 May 1896 died 5 may 1978 both are buried at Memorial Gardens Cemetery in Overton County, Curtis Vaughn married Jean Elem, Carlis born 29 March 1905 died 3 May 1905 buried at Liberty Cemetery, Carlin married Estelle (Bullock) Carmon married Fredia Clara (Bartlett), Colah D. born 3 July 1912 died 21 July 1987 married Thurman W. Averitt, Codice married Fred Speiker

Ambrose Sullivan and Lee Ann (Ray) Sullivan

Ambrose Sullivan born abt. 1821 inTN died 13 July 1908 in TN he married 4 April 1869 to Lee Ann (Ray) born abt. 1848 died aft. 1920 both are buried in the Sullivan Family Cemetery just off of the Livingston Boat Dock Road which turns off of Highway 52 going towards Celina from Livingston. Their children know are listed below however according to the 1900 Census Leeann listed she had 10 children with only 7 living. Robert Martin, William E., Mollie married Eugene Horner, Ellen married William B. Conner, Hixy married Ben Dulworth.

April 1869 Page 281, 289
State VS A. Sullivan fathered illegitimate child of Nancy J. Reynolds.

Have a copy of Ambrose Sullivan's Civil War widow's application also.
Her CW pen.#1834.Her pension was accepted. She stated in her pension that her and Ambrose had 10 children 7 living 3 males and 4 females she gives there age in her application.

1870 Census Overton Co. TN Dist.#13/74
Ambrose Sullivan 48 m TN farmer; Lean 23 f TN.

1880 Census Overton Co. TN Dist.#4/84
Ambers Sullivan 56 m TN TN NC; Lee Ann 33 f TN; Mary P. 8 f
dau. TN; WIley 6 m son; Robert M. 4 m son; Calvin D. 1 f dau..

1900 Census Overton Co. TN Dist.#4/123-126
Ambrose Sullivan w m m31 TN TN TN farmer; Lean 51 w f TN
TN TN 10-7; Ellen 17 w f Dec. 1882 dau.; William E. 15 w m May
1885 son; Robert M. 24 w m Nov. 1875 m0 son farmer; Bertha H.
21 w f Mch. 1879 dau/law.

1920 Census Overton Co. TN Dist.#7/197-197
Lee A. Sullivan 72 f mo./law living in the household of her son in
law William Conner and his wife Ellen her daughter.

Joseph Corbit Allred and Nancy J. (Stout) Allred
with son Flem Hazen Allred

Joseph Corbit Allred was born in Overton County the son of
Virgil Allred and Permelian Susan (Cantrell) Allred he married
19 February 1922 to Nancy J. (Stout) daughter of William Peyton
Stout and Ellen (Cantrell) Stout.

Cubert Tinzie Gore

He was born 15 July 1895 in Overton County died 22 February 1977 buried Crestlawn Cemetery in Putnam County TN married Verda (Ledbetter).

Matilda (Allred) Dishman

She was born 4 June 1856 in Overton County TN died 20 July 1922 buried in Seattle King County Washington and was daughter of Theophelus Allred and Elizabeth (Bowman) Allred she married 3 September 1876 in Overton County to Solomon Addison Dishman born 8 September 1854 in Overton County died9 July 1925 buried at Mt. Pleasant Cemetery King County Seattle Washington. They left Overton County after 1880 Census.

1880 Census Overton Co. TN

1900 Census Ravalli MT
He is living in the same district as his brother William J. Dishman and a nephew John W. Cantrell.

1920 Census King Co WA

Addison Dishman possibly lived in Florida about 1920.Obedia his niece
said she remembered him coming back to Overton County one time and she was married and had 2 children and he was from Florida that is the only time she can remember seeing him. I have a copy of his death certificate from the state of Montana. It gives his father as Joseph Dishman and don't give his mother's name. It tells where he is buried and gives his birth date. That is most of the information.

Kellum Cantrell and Cora B. (Ramsey) Cantrell

Kellum Cantrell born August 1876 died between 1920-1930 married 28 February 1897 to Cora B. (Ramsey) born 2 February 1878 died 13 November 1929 she is buried at the Nimville Deck Cemetery Overton County.

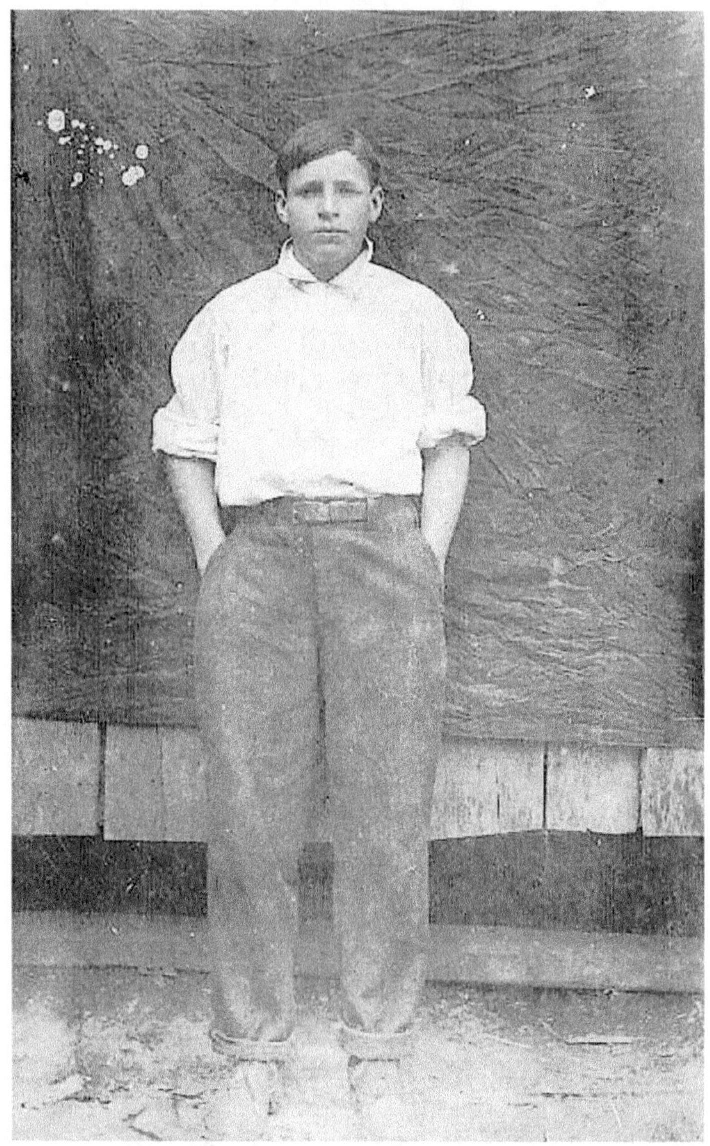

Lee Webb Cantrell

He was born 18 December 1895 died 21 November 1918 son of Kellum and Cora B. (Ramsey) Cantrell buried at the Nimville Deck Cemetery in Overton County TN. He had two sisters Della married Frank Gore and Dessie married William Frank "Willie" Hammock.

Early Photograph of the Hatcher Home

This is an early photograph of the Hatcher home located in the Hatcher Hall community of Overton County currently owned by the Keisling family. Notice the old wooden sidewalks going up to the porch.

Those in picture are thought to be Joe D. Hatcher with granddaughter Nova born about 1907 and wife not verified though. Picture would have been made between 1900 and 1910.

SECTION II
GENERAL HISTORY

Some Livingston History
By Capt., A. L. Dale

This history of the town of Livingston is written by A. L. Dale, now in his eighty-second year, and contains remembrances from his boyhood days of 1854 up to the present day, making in all some sixty-eight years. He has lived most of his life in Overton county and in that part of Clay county taken from Overton, 16 miles from Livingston.

My first visit to the town of Livingston was in August 1854, when i came to see Robertson Bros. Circus. The town was then built around the square the same shape and size as at present.

The store house of Mrs. Miller where the Overton Supply Co. is now located was then owned by the Goodbars, A. J. and J. L., who were merchants. The Farmers Bank is on the lands then owned by Doak H. Capps who had a general store. For many years before the Civil War this was the property of Judge W. W. Goodpasture, who also owned it during the war and afterwards until his death. The lands from the Farmers Bank on Depot Street to the railroad, were owned by Judge W. W. Goodpasture as well as much other land of Livingston that now has splendid brick business houses on it as well as fine dwellings and residence property.

The law office of E. C. Knight is where Col. F. H. Daugherty had a hotel building in 1854. Col. Daughtery owned all the lands on the south side of the street from the square to the branch south on the Hilham road. This part of the town is now known as the "Burks Addiction" with many good residences on Daughtery street to the railroad through the lands of the late Col. F. H. Daughtery.

The railroad runs through the Daughtery lands and the lands of Mrs. Miller formerly the Goodbar lands. The railroad depot, the Morgan Produce Co., A. J. Mofield & Co., the Maxwell-Hill Wholesale

Grocery Co. are located on land formerly owned by Judge W. W. Goodpasture.

On the Daugherty lands, in the "Burks Addition" are the homes of W. T. Goff, J. S. Fleming, Col. J. A. Hargrove, A Turley Knight and Chas P. Gray, editor to the Livingston Enterprise, from the square on the south side of the pike is E. C. Knight, Bedford Arnold, Gainsboro Telephone Co. and the Maynord Hotel. On the east side of Daugherty street, Willard Maynord, W. A. Bussell, Pleasant Smith. On the south side of the pike, going west, are Alfred Lea, Chas D. Mitchell, R. L. Little, Bob Chilton.

On the north side of the pike, going west, is the residence of Chancellor W. R. Officer, on the site of the home of the late James W. McHenry. Judge McHenry owned this property and lived on it some years before the Civil War; he was one of Tennessee's most distinguished lawyers, adjutant general under Gov. Isham G. Harris, a captain in the Confederate army. He died in Nashville in the seventies, an old man a wealthy man and one of the greatest lawyers this state has produced. On the McHenry property, also are the residences of James H. Myers, C. J. Cullom, a lawyer of the Livingston bar and a grandson of Judge Alvin Cullom, Elmo Eubank, Bob Nunally and J. G. Eastland on the lands once owned by William Pickett, who was county court clerk of Overton county form 1856 to 1862. Next building is the Light & Power Co. and Ice Plant, then J. C. Bilbrey Spoke Co., then the Livingston Heading Co., with many other business and residence buidlings in the northwest side of the town, with a railroad switch through this section.

The west side of the square is owned by Fleming & Myers Co. with a large two story brick store, then the post office and barber shop, all brick the Arnold Hardware Co. and the Citizens Bank & Trust Co., both in two story brick buildings that would be a credit to a town much larger than Livingston.

Before the Civil War the west side of the square was owned by Judge J. D. Goodpasture and Ples Armstrong, the latter a merchant until the war. Judge Goodpasture had a dwelling house on his property which later became the property of Dan Read, who ran a hotel and drug store for a number of years. The Armstrong property was a large hotel building known as the Overton Hotel, and was built by Judge J. D. Goodpasture and W. J. Wright, who died at Cookeville, Tenn., Judge Goodpasture afterwards moved to Nashville, where he died at the age of 74.

The public square is 300 feet each way. In the center is the court house, the third building of its kind but on the original foundation. The first court house was built in 1832-3 and the present buidling in 1868-9.

On the street leading, west from the square is a drug store, located on the lot where Dr. Dan Read had a livery and feed stable for a long time in the early days and later owned by Dr. Read's son-in-law, Emmet Goff. Also the residence of J. C. Bilbrey, which was first occupied by T. E. Goff, who now lives at Monterey. Next is the Commercial Hotel on the site of the first residence ever built in Livingston, by a family of the name of Cash, in 1832. Some of the Cash family still live here. James W. Cash is a grandson of the first builder of Livingston. The Commercial Hotel was first built by J. C. Bilbrey for a residence, afterwards enlarged by H. S. Estes, who converted it into a hotel, and is now owned by his widow, Mrs. L. E. Estes. H. S. Estes died many years ago; he was banker and successful business man and with Moses Miller, established the first ever in Livingston. On this street is also the Overton county jail, a large two story building of native stone. On the south side of this street in the christian church, a large house on land that William Goodbar donated to the church many years before the Civil War. Further on are many mills and residence buildings, some of them on lands once owned by Joseph Lacy, who was an old settler from East Tennessee, a tailor by trade, who had learned the work under President Andrew Johnson at Greenville when both were young men. Also on the Lacy property is a large saw and planing mill run by M. H. Hankins, who is also a contractor and builder.

Going out from the square, north on the Celina road is the "Hankins Addition" consisting of many handsome residences located on lands once owned by A. A. Swope, who was a lawyer here for years before the Civil War. Later he moved to Carthage where he died.

On the north side of the square is the Parks Grocery, some vacant lots from which the buildings were burned a few years ago, and a large brick garage. From this point the street leads to Livingston Academy, in the north part of the town, passing by the Livingston Roller Mill and many beautiful dwellings.

Livingston Academy is one of the best high schools in the state. It has nearly 1,000 pupils and more than 20 teachers and is run under the supervision of the C. W. B. M. of the Christian church. It is located on lands owned by the Armstrongs and McHenrys before the Civil War. At the time the school was established these lands were owned by Gov. A. H. Roberts, Miss Willie Harris, J. H. Estes and perhaps others. The school owns the valuable property, has nice modern buildings and splendid equipment.

On the east side of this street is the Methodist church, a large two story brick building. On the corner is the large store house of M. F. Marcom and the Dixie Theatre, a moving picture house. Between the church and these buildings is the law office of F. D. White and a barber shop and a restaurant, all brick and formerly the old jail building. On the site of the Marcom store, a Mr. Roberts ran a hotel in the early days. He was the father of Capt. J. S. Roberts, of the Confederate army, who was later circuit court clerk for many years.

On the street leading east and passing this corner is the Brown Hotel and many nice residences, among them being that of Capt. T.F. Stephens, who commanded a company in the late war and is now postmaster, and Mrs. Nora Dale, present county register and widow of the late R. A. Dale, who was register at the time of his death. These residences are on land once owned by John Hall, an early settler and a Mexican soldier, who was one of the largest property owners of his day.

The east side of the square is solidly built with brick and metal business houses and law offices of C. J. Cullom, Mayor B. H. Hunt, Judge W. R. Officer, County Superintendent Geo. O. Lea and others. Gov. A. H. Roberts formerly had offices over the store of Miss Madge Barnes. This property was formerly owned by J. B. Hereford, Capt.

A. L. Windle and Dr. David Graham. Nearby was the harness and saddle shop of Mr. James Smith and the general work shop of Phillip Myers.

Going east on the State Highway from the Farmers Bank is the Roberts House, formerly the residence of Judge W. W. Goodpasture, who had the house built about 1854. The builder was Mr. James Estes, who came here from East

Tennessee and built many of the older houses in Livingston. He was a good man and died here only a few years ago at the advanced age of 93. This was the first house he built here and was considered the finest residence in this entire section

In its day Goodpasture lands. Then the home of Dr. M. J. Qualls residence and office is next and both buildings are on Rev. John T. Wilson; then the home of Mrs. Barnes, widow of the late Capt. J. A. Barnes, of the Confederate army and one of the leading lawyers of his day; then the home of Mrs. Mary Windle, widow of Capt. A. L. Windle, who was a merchant for many years located on the present site of the B. & O. Drug Store. Then the Baptist church On the left of the State Highway, east of the square, the large brick residence of Dr. A. B. Qualls, the offices of Dr. Qualls and Attorney E. A. Qualls, on land formerly owned by Judge W. W. Goodpasture. Then the office and residence of Dr. J. D. Capps, formerly owned by his father Dr. M. B. Capps, and on the site of the old Presbyterian Church. Then Phillip Myers, John Miller and R. L. Mitchell Jr. conclude the residences to the bridge near Burr Specks residence.

On the street north from the State Highway, at this point are many beautiful residences on lands that were once owned by the McHenrys and later by the Armstrongs. This property changed hands several times within a few years and finally became the property of Gov. A. H. Roberts and is now owned by a company.

Joining these lands is a large boundary of land that was once owned by Jefferson Goodpasture and later by Judge W. W. Goodpasture and is now considered among the most desirable residence property of the town. It contains some fine residences owned by prosperous men. Among them are J. T. Lansden, T. B. Copeland, James Bilbrey, a Confederate veteran, Cooper W. Henson; S. J. Bilbrey, Squire F. G. Deck, Dr. Zachry, George Boswell and others.

Many beautiful residences are on lands once owned by Elisha Chastain and by Jefferson Goodpasture before him.

South of the town, along the State Highway and near it, are many beautiful residences. Among them is that of Capt.,C. E. Myers, which is one of the most beautiful homes in this section. Capt. Myers is in his 93rd year he is a veteran of the Mexican War, marched into Mexico City with Gen. Winfield Scott in 1847, and is the sole survivor in Tennessee of that war. He organized and commanded the first company of Confederate soldiers that went out from Overton county and he saw hard service during the whole of the war.

Further along the State Highway, on both sides, are many beautiful residences the owners of which I will not try to name. Readers of this history may find some mistakes as it is hard to give such a detailed statement from memory. But as a native born Overton countian, 82 years of age, and acquainted with the town of Livingston 68 years, living in the town most of the time for 43 years, and knowing all the parties named in this history, I feel safe in saying that it is very nearly correct. The writer of this history has been in the hotel business most of the time since 1884 and was well acquainted with the town many years before the Civil War. I was a Confederate soldier from this county and was sworn in on the public square at Livingston on the 5th day of September 1861 and surrendered at Carthage, Tenn. on the 23rd day of May 1865. I am a son of William Dale, who lived on Obed's River, Overton county, Tennessee, and a grandson of William Dale, who was a soldier under General (afterwards President) Andrew Jackson at New Orleans in 1812.

The writer had five other brothers who were Confederate soldiers; and best of all the whole generation of the Dales always were and now are Democrats and all that are now living, both men and women, will go to the polls on August 3rd and vote for Benton McMillin for Governor. And further than that, they will all support the Democratic nominees in November and expect to help to return Cordell Hull to his seat in Congress, where he rightfully belongs.

A.L. Dale

Livingston, Tenn.
July 22, 1922.

Capt. Dale's interesting article was handed in before the late primary election, in which his and our friend, Benton McMillin, was defeated for Governor. On account of its length and the fact that we were crowded with political advertising, it was necessarily omitted until now. All of it, except the reference to Gov. McMillin's candidacy, is as new now as then.

1930's Livingston Fire Chief Millard Hawkins

Livingston Town Square North Side 1940's

Holman's Dry Good Store on West Side of Square in Livingston
where the Paper Place is at present time

Herman Holman Dry Good Store 1953

Miller building about 1920 South Side of Square
next to Post Office

Alpine Institute Miller Hall building

Alpine Church about 1938

East Side of Livingston Square believed to be where
Eye Centers of Tennessee is at present time

East Side of Square…corner building is where Savage Law Office
is presently located (circa 1912). Notice dirt streets and rail fence
around courthouse yard.

Doctor Jacob M Shelton

Article written December 21 ,1888 information pertaining to J. M Shelton says that where he now lives 2 lines illegible of Monroe as the Williams Hotel where Honorable Adam M. Totten, Sam Tourney Judge, Jas Quarles, William Cullom and a host of bright lights of Uncle Billy and Aunt Jenny as they were called. The Dr. has in his house enough curiosities picked up in the county to interest and no matter where from that they may pass and it is a pleasure for him to show and explain. In the corner close to the fire he has his lately captured rattler all snuggly put away for the winter. He has lately taken time to rebuild the east chimney to the old house and I must say that the workmanship is fine. In the back as the copeing the Dr. has had put in a beautiful place of white marble with the following inscription "Built for J. M. Shelton by David L. Sells, 1888". In the center is cut in good style the square and compose the emblems of the ancient Order of Free and accepted Masons. Behind this marble is laid a complete history of all inhabitants of Monroe and also giving the dates of many things that happened in and around Monroe.

Other information on Dr. Shelton says that he practiced medicine for a number of years in the Monroe area also operated a general store and was very active in the work of the fraternal order. He moved to Bushnel Florida and died there in 1915. He as was a charter member of the Livingston Lodge No. 302, the I.O.O.F. was organized October 18, 1900 J. M. Shelton was listed. The Knights of Pythias Livingston Lodge No. 195 was chartered October 8, 1904 Dr. Shelton was one of the charter members.

A letter was found in the time capsule in the chimney that was opened in 1988 by the owners of the home in Monroe at that time. Several things had survived the 100 years since being placed in the capsule in 1888. One was a letter that stated J. M. Shelton was born in November 23, 1844 in Washington Co. VA. Some of the other items found are showed below calling cards at that time or business cards as they are called now.

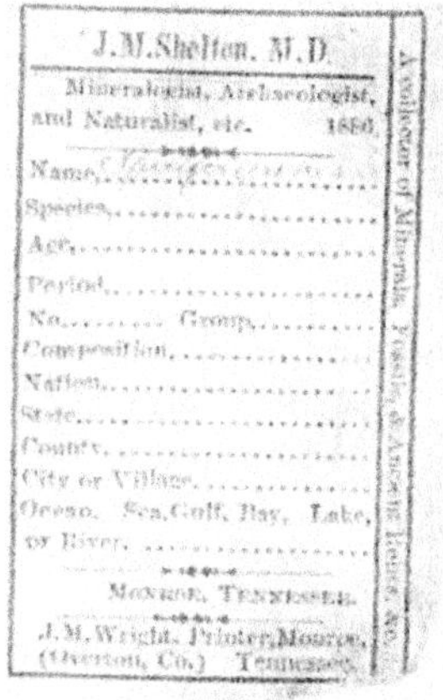
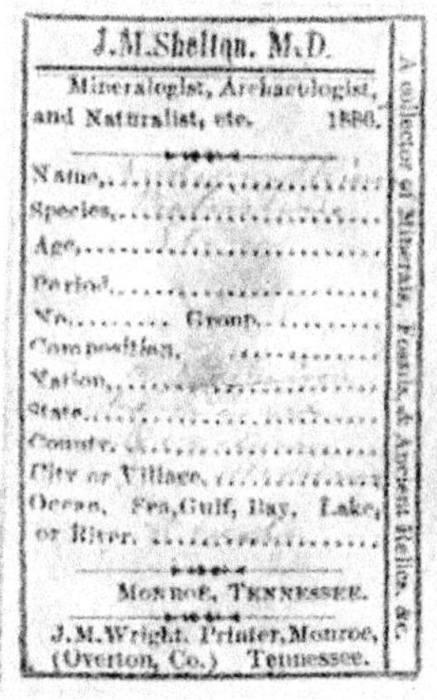
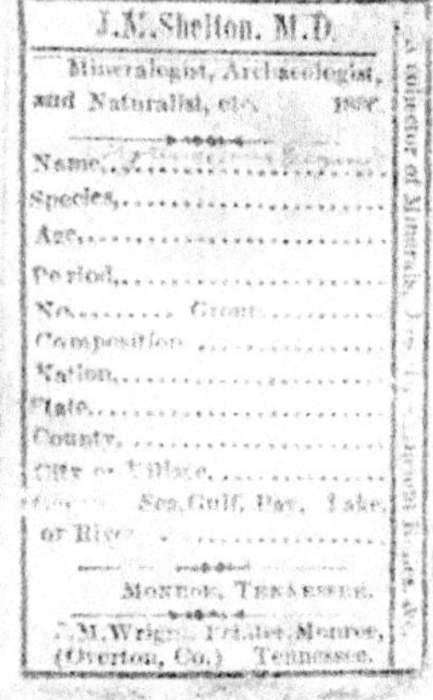

Note at the bottom of the card J.M. Wright Printer, Monroe Overton Co. Tennessee

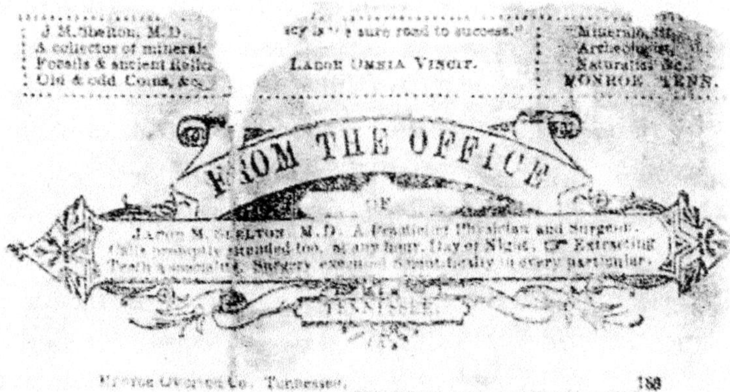

April 27, 1927 Article of Early Civic Club

Civic Club Elect Officers

The Woman's Civic Club of Livingston. Tenn. met in its regular session April 15, 1927, and elected the officers for another year, as follows:

Pres.. Mrs. J. T. Lansden: Vice Pres., Mrs. J. S. Fleming; Treas., Mrs. E. C. Knight; Secy., Mrs. M. H. Hankins. Mrs. Lansden was elected as deligate to the State Convention in Nashville in May and Mrs. Phebe E. Clark alternate.

The following report was submitted to headquarters:

We have twelve active members and fifty-eight associated members. We have made our anual contributions as follows.

To Alumni Association of the blind. Chattanooga, Tenn. $ 5.00

To Students Loan Fund, 10.00
To Tuberculosis seals, 3.00
To Maintainance Fund, 1.00
To Federation dues, 4.00
To Flowers, 30.00

Total $53.20
To cash on hands $681.10

The club has served dinners for the local Exchange Club and has cleared $362.70 on these dinners this year. We hope to be able to purchase us a club house during the next year. We expect to broaden our work each year.

By Secy.

Older view of the courthouse in Livingston looking from what seems like northwest side

HISTORY OF LIVINGSTON/OVERTON COUNTY
Written by Calvin E. Myers age 94 Nov. 1924
Taken from files at T.S.L.A.

Livingston, Tenn
Dec. 2nd 1924
Mr. A. H. Roberts
Nashville, Tenn

Dear Sir and friend:

I recd your letter a few days ago, was glad to hear from you and appreciate your kind wishes, now in reply to your letter will say I knew James Chisum and John Gore when I was only a boy but I remember they were very prominent men in Overton Co. am sorry I can not tell you more of them I enclose a history of Overton Co of its first settlement up to the present you can look over this history and turn it over to John Trotwood Moore 2nd State Librian this history was written for a Mr. J. B. Lea he wrote me for some but when it reached the address he gave me he was not there Thinking you would like to have it for one of State Treasures.

With best wishes for you and family

I remain your old friend

C. E. Myers

By Daughter Maggie

History Letter

Livingston Tenn

Nov. 6 1924

Mr. J. B. Lea

Murfressboro Tenn

Dear Sir:

Received your letter and will give you the best information of Overton Co I can, First I will have to give you a history of Jackson co. before I can give a comprehensive history of Overton Co. Jackson Co. when first formed contained perhaps as many sq miled as R. I.. The first courts in Jackson Co were held in what was known as the Hickie house two miles north of Monroe which is now in Overton Co. then moved from there to Bachelor Jim Brown farm on Flat Creek which was a very common log house about 24 X 24 feet. James Cook who was my mothers first husband was the first sheriff of Jackson Co. Later under Gov. Blunt's administration the courts were again moved to fort Blunt which was later called Williamsburg was again moved by vote of the people to Gainsboro which is the present Co. seat of Jackson Co.

The following counties were taken from the original Jackson Co. namely Overton Co. Fentress Co. Putnam Co. Picketts Co. Clay Co. First court held in Overton was at Monroe and moved by vote of the people to Livingston the boundaries of Overton

Co. are Putnam on west Clay Co. on north, Pickett Co on east, southern boundry being white co. Overton Co has made some very substantial improvments one worthy of mention being a pike recently built which extend from Pickett Co. via Livingston to Putnam Co. also a cross pike by way of Alpine Livingston to Clay Co. line Livingston is situated in the fertile valley about one by two miles surrounded by beautiful mountain scenery a population of about three thousand people.

Livingston has a college which has an annual enrollment of from three to six hundred students just completed a public school building costing thirty thousand dollars have a nine months school attended by about three hundred children. Have two banks, two large Hdw houses, four dry goods stores, four hotels, and three drug stores. Have telephone and electric light system, Have a commodious court house built of brick situated in the square surrounded by substantial brick buildings occupied by the various business firms Livingston has six Doctors, The T. K. & N. rail road extend from Livingston intersecting the Tenn. central at Algood and is said to do the largest business per mileage of any road in the United States, a vast amount of timber being shiped out, especialy telephone poles and hard wood lumber Livingston is second largest shipping center of poultry in the state, being also the main distributing center of the intermountain country. I believe this is a few of the most important changes taken place which I have told from memory and trusting will be of interest to you.

Yours very truly

C. E. Myers

Age 94 yrs.

HIGH POINTS IN HISTORY OF
OVERTON COUNTY, TENN.

By C. C. Justus
Taken from *Nashville Banner*

Overton county was erected in 1806 from a part of Jackson county and was named in honor of Judge John Overton, the most intimate friend of Andrew Jackson at that time. The county is bounded on the north by Clay and Pickett, on the south by Putnam, on the east by Pickett and Fentress, on the west by Jackson and Clay counties. It has an area of 376 square miles, is drained by the Obed and the Roaring rivers, tributaries to the Cumberland. The county is hilly and fertile, has good timber in all parts, good coal deposits. The county has fifteen caves of a notable class; these are, Garrett's cave and Rock Shelter, Saltpeter [three of this name], Wash Lee, Crawford, Allen, Quares, Quarles Rock Shelter, Falling Water, Pine Hill, Wolfe Branch, Breir Hill, and Peter Caves. The largest of these are the Saltpeter No. 101, Wolfe Branch, Crawford and Falling Water caves. Some of these have widths of over 200 feet, and lengths from 600 to 1,000 feet. The characteristics are the same as those of the other counties of this group.

Excellent grazing lands are found in all parts of the county. This results in much cattle and sheep asa a part of the leading productions. Corn, wheat, hay and live stock are the chief sources of incomes to the farmers.

The earliest settlers were Col. Stephen Copeland and his son, "Big Joe" Copeland. Others were: John Goodpasture, father of the distinguished jurist, Judge Jefferson D. Goodpasture, Capt. Jesse Arnold, Capt. Simeon Hinds, father of the learned chemist and teacher, Dr. J. I. D. Hinds of Lebanon; Benjamin Totten, father of A. W. O. Totten; Moses Fisk, Judge Alvin Cullom, Gen. William Cullom, Adam Hunsman, and some descendants of John Sevier. "Big Joe" Copeland was the outstanding man for stature, being seven feet tall, wighing 350 pounds. His sister was the first white child born within the borders of Overton county. This on Mathis creek near Windle, four miles south of Livingston. The father of "Big Joe" was from

Virginia. "Big Joe" was a giant, physically and above the average mentally. One of the sisters married Henry Dillon, who settled near Livingston. Among her descendants is John M. Dillon, a prosperous farmer; also W. H. Dillon.

"Big Joe" Copeland acquired a large body of fertile lands including the Copeland Cove. He had five sons, whose names ended with the same letters – Richardson, a captain in the Mexican war; Harrison; Wilkerson, Addison and Ellison. All these were large men. Some of the descendants of Harrison are yet in the county. One of these is Thomas Carr Copeland of the Alpine section of the county. Joseph M. Copeland, son of Captain Richardson and grandson of "Big Joe", also resides in the Alpine community, and is the father of Thomas B., cahier of the Citizens Bank & Trust Co. of Livingston and actively engaged in the manufacture of lumber and other lines of business. In his palmy days, "Big Joe" had fights and was too clever for any antagonist. A bully in Virginia who had whipped all comers in his section of the state, heard of "Big Joe", and came all the way through on horseback after he had send forward his challenge to the giant. When he arrived and looked over this celebrated giant of Overton, who looked down from an eminence of seven feet, he withdrew his challenge, Copeland cracked walnuts between his teeth.

Capt. Richardson Copeland was a veteran of two wars; he was captain in both the Mexican and the civil wars.

Jefferson Goodpasture settled at Livingston and John G. Goodpasture settled near Hilham, the oldest town of the county, eight miles west of Livingston. Hilham was settled when the territory was yet a part of North Carolina. Both were active, well-to-do farmers and slave holders. Some of their descendants remained in Overton county, while many went away. John reared fourteen children and gave each a good education. His sons were profesional men. Judge Jefferson D. was a noted jurist and accumulated much property for his day. He moved to Nashville where he had law and real estate offices late in the seventies. He was the father of Rev. John Ridley Goodpasture, an able Presbyterian minister, now of McMinnville, Tenn. Another son Albert V. is a resident of Montgomery County, a historian of note, and is the owner of a large plantation. He served a number of years as clerk of the Supreme Court at Nashville. He was Colaborator with the late Capt. W. R. Garrett in the authorship of a history of Tennessee that was used extensively in the schools of the state, being one of the books adopted by the text book commission. Will Henry, another, was deputy Supreme Court clerk for many years, also was in the book business in Nashville. Dillard G. Jr., is a prosperous business man in Nashville, Winburn W. was an attorney of recognized ability and a successful business man who died at Livingston in 1910 at an advanced age. Both J. D. and W. W. served as clerk and master of the chancery court at Livingston when they were young lawyers. M. G. was a physician and had a large practice at Cookeville at his death. Attorney-General E. H. Boyd, of Cookeville is a grandson of the later Doctor Goodpasture mentioned above.

On of the older daughterrs of John Goodpasture married William Dale and lived across the river in what is now Clay County. She had a large family and five or more of her sons enlisted in the Confederate army. One of these, Capt. Jack Dale, was killed in battle. A. L., another son is now 85 years old and resides at Livingston. He is proprietor of the Commercial hotel, well preserved, mentally and physically, and is one of the five who cast their lot with the "Lost Cause". A. V. and J. R. Goodpasture were graduates of the University of Tennessee. One daughter of John G. married Dennis Mitchell and left two sons. One of these, John M. D. was attorney-general for the Fifth circuit for many years, and was such at his death. I. W. Mitchell's son, John Ridley Mitchell, was formerly attorney-general. He was appointed by Governor Peay to succeed Judge E. C. Snodgrass as circuit judge, when the latter entered the Court of Appeals. Two other sons of I. W. Mitchell are W. W. a live stock dealer, and Dr. Elmo, a prominent physician of Cookeville. A daughter Mrs. Hettie Rose Speck, is the wife of B. L. Speck of Livingston.

Capt. Calvin E. Myers the last surviving veteran in the state of the Mexican war, was born and reared at Fort Blount in Jackson county, but he has lived in Overton since reaching manhood; has been a citizen of Livingston for fifty years or more. After returning from the Mexican war he married in Macon County an aunt of Judge

Sam M. Young of Dixon Springs. She was a sister of Addison Young and the late Mrs. J. W. Richardson, related of the Young's of Sparta. Captain Myers has been a farmer, mechanic and merchant. He is now 96 years old and alert mentally and otherwise. He is a man of engaging manners, a pleasing personality, enjoys host of friends to whom he lends the sunshine and bids them overlook the shadows. He was a captain in two wars, the Mexican and the civil. Captain Myers had a brother, Luther, two years his senior, who died a few years since. He was also a captain two wars - his last captaincy being in the Confederate army. Captain Calvin Myers, now surviving at 96 has a son Calvin, in the same town aged 76.

One of the notable and lovable citizens of Livingston is Hon. R. L. Mitchell of the internal revenue service, whose office is in the Knoxville custom house. Mr. Mitchell was 25 years a county official, having served five and a half years as clerk and master in chancery court, and twenty years as clerk of the county court. J. O. Collins sheriff for sixteen years, was elected one time over M. C. Bilbrey. John Hart Jr. a descendant of the Culloms, is a genial optimist and is serving his second term as circuit clerk.

This great country is the home of the Culloms, whose history is familiar to those interested in good and useful citizenship. Richard Cullom, father of the late governor and United States senator, went to Illinois. The family originally came from Monticello, Ky., to Overton county. Edward N. settled at Monroe, Overton county, and was the father of twenty-four children by one wife. There were triplets and twins in this family. James Cullom settled at Union City, Obion county. He was the grandfather of the reporter of opinions of the Supreme court. William C. Cullom was a Methodist class leader for fifty-six years; was a great orator and a member of congress for two terms; a contemporary of President Polk and made a sensational campaign against the late John H. Savage. William C. went from Livingston to Gainsboro, then to Carthage, then to Clinton, where he died in 1896, aged 85. He had two sisters, Mrs. Spencer McHenry and Mrs. Lucinda Hart who died at the age of eighty, grandmother of John Hart to whom reference has been made as the present clerk of the Overton Circuit court. These were residents of the county when is was organized. The descendants of Mrs. Hart are John Hart Jr., Mrs. J. B. Dale, and Miss Willie Harris, the latter now private secretary to Congressman Cordell Hull.

The descendants of Alvin Cullom are W. J. Cullom, Bob Cross Cullom, Young Cullom, Mrs. A. C. Terry and Charles J. Cullom, a prominent lawyer of Livingston. William B. Armstrong, a great grandson of William C. Cullom, is a dentist and has a brother, Walter a successful farmer, Spencer McHenry another descendant of the Culloms is cashier of the Fourth and First National Bank of Nashville, and is a grandson of Creed Huddleston of Mexican war fame.

Mention should be made of R. L. Mitchell, great grandson of Robert L. who settled in the western part of the county when it was part of North Carolina. He enlisted in the war of 1812. Attorney Arthur Mitchell of Knoxville is a descendant. The father of R. L. Mitchell, of the revenue service, died in the Confederate army in 1862.

W. C. Cullom had twin sons, Henry Clay and Daniel Webster, the latter while visiting Shelby M. in Illinois at the opening of the civil war, joining the Federal army; Henry Clay at home joined, the Confederate army. Susan Cullom one of the brilliant women of the county went to Illinois and became the wife of Alfred Phillips.

Livingston is the home of former Governor Albert H. Roberts, and a thriving town of 1,200 people; it is the terminus of the Tennessee, Kentucky & Northern Railway, a branch of the Tennessee Central. The town has two banks, two weekly newspapers and several manufacturing establishments. The first court was held at a place later called Jones' Store, about five miles north of Livingston, and became a rival for the honor of being the county seat. An election in 1832 resulted favorably to Livingston. Hilham, founded in 1805 is the oldest town, Moses Fisk was its founder. The Fisk Female Academy was located there, the first school distinctly for girls chartered in the South, and one of the first in the United States.

The railway mileage is thirty. There are six high and 84 elementary schools. The tax values for 1921 was $4,471,888. The county has enviable record for notable men in every great period of civic and industrial life.

NASHVILLE GRAIN DEALER
FORMER OVERTON COUNTY BOY
HAS MANY RECOLLECTIONS

J. A. Daugherty writes interesting letter to the Enterprise About visit to Hundreth Birthday Celebration and Home Coming

By J. A. Daugherty

Born within a stone throw of the court house at Livingston, 70 years ago, I welcomed the priviledge of visiting the old home town on the occasion of the celebration of its 100th anniversary, August 10, and witnessing the great influx of people coming with the hope of meeting relatives, friends and school mates of long ago.

A flood of sweet memories were awakened within me, when I met and clasped hands with men and women I knew when a child, but had not seen for 50 or 60 years.

My sympathies for the able speakers on the program were truly sincere. Under the tent, which was packed to standing capacity could not accomodate one third of the crowd, the heat was terrific and the audience so intent upon seeking relatives and friends were talking and mingling in such confusion, that it was impossible for the speakers to obtain respectful hearing. No man can speak with satisfaction under such conditions.

The discomfort of the tent forced me to retire to that comfortable front porch at the Roberts Hotel, where I enjoyed that thrilling delight of a real reunion of relatives, schoolmates and friends, and also a most bountiful dinner, well and deliciously prepared which would charm the appetite of the most critical epicure.

The information compiled for this occasion regarding Overton county and Livingston was very interesting. It disclosed the identity of those courageous and determined men who settled in a wilderness about 150 years ago men of vision, bravery, and determination, who builded a foundation on the basis of church, Christianity, and the little red schoolhouse, which made for character forming that has gone down through the succeeding generations and will continue throughout all time.

From this influence Overton county has produced men who have gone into nearly every state in this Union, lawyers, preachers, doctors, teachers, business men, and farmers who have made good.

The contribution of Overton county to the affairs of Tennessee is one Governor and countless Congressmen that have made records for honesty and purpose.

Overton county has always done its full duty in times of war and has sent volunteer soldiers to every war since its formation as a county and rightfully boasts of a fine war record.

Overton county has played no little part in the affairs of the good old U.S.A.. Its latest contribution to the goverment is its Secretary of State, Cordell Hull, an outstanding statesmen, who has recently demonstrated his ability to meet on equal terms the greatest minds the shrewdest diplomats of the civilized world making him and outstanding international figure and Cordell Hull an Overton county boy will go down in history as one of the great statesmen of his day.

My observation is that Overton county has not sent to other states its most valuable men as the record might imply. I find Overton county holds today and has always held men of strength and character evidenced by the fact that in all these 100 years of existence. I am told that not one Overton county official has defaulted and there has never been a bank failure in Livingston. The funds of the county and on individuals deposited in Livingston banks have always been safeguarded by men of honor and integrity.

For this wonderful record we are justly proud but we must give credit where credit is due and to those pioneers who started us on the right road to success and character building we should ever be feel grateful.

But my deductions are that we are neglecting to give the proper consideration to the real power behind the throne.

The development of worthy men could not have materialized without the great influence. The hand that rocks the cradle rules the world and the noble women of each generation have been the real power in character building down through following generations throughout. Women have put the finishing touches to all great undertakings if they succeeded.

My personal knowledge of course goes back no further than my childhood 70 years ago and I cannot testify for women before that time but my belief is that women have been the balancing power in all ages of civilization.

My memory when a boy at Livingston brings before me a beautiful picture. A stately Judge Alvin Cullom driving into town in his carriage his wife a sweet little white haired woman more active and alert than the judge himself helping guide and comfort him. I remember dear old Aunt Cindy Hart and Uncle John Hart her husband whom everybody loved I call to mind cousin Polly Armstrong who had a house full of boys and girls of her own but her hospitable home was always open to the entire countryside. I shall never forget two dear old ladies Mrs. Keeton and Mrs. Henson. They tolerated us little town rats that during the summer season we made the welkin ring with water battles and swimming in their fish ponds. They treated us always with kindness and consideration which made its imprint. And Aunt dear old mother Hall the Seth Parker of her day. Her house was always open to the young people for the community singing and cousin Hennie Capps who came from prominent Officer family who were then and have always been prominent in the affairs of Overton county a better women with more influence for good never lived. And Aunt Rhoda Estes who lived next the schoolhouse and mothered every boy and girl in town but made us walk a chalk line.

Cousin Lee Ann Colquitt and Mrs. Draper were women of great influence for good with the young boys and girls.

Mrs. Turner living next door to my home with a house full of boys and girls did much toward the development of the rising generation. One of the thrills of my visit was meeting her three daughters at this homecoming girls, I had played with as children gone to school and to mother Hall's singings together. They are all prominent in social civic circles where they live.

Another active intelligent good women much younger than those already mentioned but a power for good still lives but for five years has confined to her bed a result of an unfortunate fall, breaking her hip. She is the same cheerful unselfish good woman she has always been never a complaint or the least resentment against her fate, and it is a blessed privilege to visit her and bask in the sunlight of her sweet cheerfulness. She is one of the friends of my childhood and many Overton county people will remember her as a resident of Livingston and love as I do, Aunt Ella Cullom.

My belief is that these good women did much more for the development of the generation to follow than did the men of whom we are so justly proud.

With sadness I remember many of my schoolmates that have passed on to their reward. But I am thankful for the privilege of again meeting so many at this homecoming who are yet active and valuable citizens.

A real thrill was given me when I met a fine old gentlemen who all his life has lived in Overton county and done his part to make it a place worthy of a home for anybody in which to live. With affectionate memory of him a rawboned active sturdy boy ready for a fight a footrace or a Sunday school picnic. It was Cooper Deck my boyhood friend whom I had not seen for over 60 years. Looking back to my boyhood days I see a fat round-faced rosy cheeked boy always smiling good naturedly making everybody love him. He has given his life's work to his county and state and I hear has a son traveling in the footsteps of his honoured father and bids fair to outstrip the old man my life long friend dear old Dick Mitchell.

I regret that I was unable to find Judge Lee Bohanon I remember when Lee came to Livingston to enter school. He was about that when a boy thinks himself a man. Dear old Lee made good and was popular in very little time he has been there ever since for he married the prettiest little girl in Livingston after I left and has given his services to the upbuilding of his county and home town. Was delighted to meet my boyhood friend Jim Lacey Sorry that I missed seeing Phillip Myers another lifelong resident of Livingston. One of my pleasant memories is watching the beautiful shavings curl up in poetic rhythm from his hand pushed plane in his father's carpenter shop and listening to the friendly gibes and interesting stories of his father Uncle Cal.. He loved the boys and the boys loved Uncle Cal and Phillip.

My efforts to find my old friend Jim Henson were disappointing. I remember him as a handsome young man riding into town on a fine saddle horse and the friend of men, women children and even negroes. He has contributed much to the upbuilding of his town and county and I regret I did not see him.

I cannot let this opportunity pass to mention one other man who In my opinion did as much for the rising generations as any one person I refer to Prof. Alvin Capps who taught every worthwhile girl and boy in his schools in Livingston and other parts of that section of the country. He planted the principals of correct thinking and gave us the rudimentary basis of education. Professor Capps as we called him will live forever perhaps unsung and unseen but his influence will live forever on down through the generations that have followed and generations to come.

A marked improvement was noticed in respect to the town and conveniences. When I was a boy Livingston was not greater in population than 350 or 400. It was far removed from rail roads and it took four days of hard driving to reach Nashville from Livingston, two days to gather a load of merchandise and four days to return to Livingston ten days for the trip. I ate breakfast in Nashville drove to Livingston in 2 ½ hours spent the day in Livingston and ate my supper in Nashville all in one day.

Speaking of the importance of women I have now in mind a latter day Livingston girl a descendant of that lovely old couple Uncle John and Aunt Cindy Hart. If anybody thinks Willie Harris is only a stenographer taking dictation from the Secretary of State they have another think coming. Much of the details of that office are left to her and she handles them with efficiency diplomacy and dispatch. She has made herself so valuable that the Government sent her to London as secretary to the head of the American delegation to the World Conference.

Don't tell me women are not most important beings on God's footstool.

OVERTON COUNTY IN RE: INDIANS
By: Albert R. Hogue

Jamestown TN

A petition to the Tennessee Legislature in 1813 of over 200 men who of course were early settlers in Overton county shows the volunteer spirit for which Tennessee is noted.

The petition which appears in American Historical Magazine in July 1902 issue is here copied.

Petition of Inhabitants of Overton County 1813

To the Honorable General Assembly of the State of Tennessee now in session:

The petition of the subscribers, inhabitants of the County of Overton humbly showeth that they feel disposed to have a part in the present war with his Britannic Majesty's savage allies , viz: the Creek Nation of Indians, and conceiving they can render greater service to the United States as mounted men than they could possibly do on foot do humbly request that your honorable body would pass a law authorizing Colonel Stephen Copeland of said county to raise by voluntary enlistment a force of 500 mounted men out of the 3rd judcial circuit in said State, to march against the said nation of Indians or other tribes of the savage foe, and fight them in their own savage way and act as rangers, etc., so long as it may appear necessary and that the said voluntary force when so raised may be paid and allowed the same pay for their services as other mounted men are allowed in the service of the United States on similar occasions and that the senators and representatives in the Congress of the United States be instructed to cause the said act when passed by your honorable body to be sanc_____ by the national legislature. etc.

And your Petitioners shall ever pray, etc. B. Totten.

Jas. McCampbell, Moore Matlock, James Finley, Willie Huddleston, Thos. Livingston, Isaac Gunter, Benjamin Parrott, Samuel Miller, Thos. Burford, Joseph Campbell, John Stockton, Robt. Adkinson, John Miller, Philip Weaver, Arthur Mitchell, William Upton, William McCormick, John Carr, John Walker, Cornelius McCormick, Arthur Babb, John Hughes, Wm. Fleming, Benjamin Brown, James Harris, Jon. Kennedy, Elijah Rogers, John Sisco, Michael Speck, John R. Nelson, James Boswell, James Smith, Stephen Horn, Sam Brown, Jacob Swallows, Zachariah Eldridge, John Hammock, William Copeland, James, Copeland, Stephen Irons, Henry Dillon, Samuel Dillon, William Allen, James McBotts, Simon Flynn, James Bradshaw, Sampson Eldridge, John Eldridge, Thompson Gardenhire, Richad Boston, Samuel Dodson, William Upton, Peter Arnett, Jesse Ashburn, Thomas McDonald, Seven Alley, Joseph Rancy, William Boswell, James Lee, Jas. Officer, Phillip Upton, Thomas Jones, Tutlow Lamb, Jacob Davie, Holland Henron, Cornelius Carmack, Isaac Hosser, William Stewart, Edmond Crawford, Henry Gore, Isa Roe, John Lee, Robert Sarsa, Andew Swallows, Stephen Mayfield, James Mayfield, Jack West, Isaac Taylor, Richard Matthews, Nelson Ray, Henry Gilmore, William Taylor, Hall Dilling, Ernstort Walker, Merrell Little, William Marlow, Joel Parker, David Stuart.

Jos. M. Windle, Wm. Evans, Isaiah Ruckman, Wm. Allred, Solomon Allred, Isaac V. Hooser, Britton Smith, James Parks, Joshua Morrison, Samuel Callihan, Francis Chaney, Alex Matney, Larkin Cox, James Key, Abner Fulfer, William Cooksey, Patrick Pool, Ephraim Wyckoff, John Workman, Robert Dale, Peter Bilyue, John Maxwell, Isaac Cunningham, Jesse Gentry, Thos. Gallion, Wm. Dale, Matthew Dale, Thomas Chambless, Hardy Hunicutt, James Maxwell.

The above names the last 33 were writen by me Jos. H. Windle, at a general muster by their requests.

Mason Kelly, W. Harrison, John Patrick, Stephen Sewell, John Graham, Charles Staples, Greenwood Harrison, Carter Dalton, Joseph Harris, David Harris, Jesse Hull, John Huddleston, Allen Brock, John Cannon, John Cargile, James Zachery, John Grimsley, Joel Brock, Gideon Thomas, James Mayberry, Daniel Cannon, Isaac Shell, Wm. Gunnels, John Erwin, Martin Grimsley, Verdimon Lee, Wm. Prat, Arthur Flowers, John Harris, John Goode, Benjamin Flowers, James Barnes, Benjamin Harrison, Daniel Erwin, Fras. McConnell, Arthur Mitchell, Arthur Babb, James Willard.

Robert Boyd, Abraham Goodpasture, Joseph Grammer, Sterling Collier, George Moore, Wm. Holeman, Madison Fisk, Solomon Eaves, Randall Murray, John Smart, James McRoberts, David Lyles, James Woods, Daniel Lyles, Stephen Row, Henry Wood, Isaiah Wood, Jacob Rook, John Davice, William Dobbs, George Gilpatrick, Henry Bailey, Jeremiah Holeman, William Officer, Walter Fisk, Tony Harp, Eli Harrison, Achilles Stephens, Elijah Davis, Joel Gain, Thos. R. Harris, John Rolls, Thos. Masters, John W. Moore, John Goodpasture, John Savage, Reuben Watt, Arthur Goodpasture, John McCord, William Willard, Samuel Harris, Isham Johnson, James Murray, James McConnell, Isaac Holeman, Jesse Masters.

Read in the House of Representatives and sent to the Senate Oct. 26, 1813. Considered by the Senate the following day and laid on the table.

NATIVE SONS RETURN TO CELEBRATE LIVINGSTON'S 100ᵀᴴ ANNIVERSARY
8,000 Witness Program Thursday Depicting Overton's Century of Progress

By Tom Fuqua
(Staff Correspondent)
Taken from *Nashville Tennessean* Aug. 10 1933

Livingston, Tenn., Aug. 10

A town that was born in the hills of Tennessee when Andrew Jackson was president celebrated its 100th birthday today.

And on its centennial celebration, back to Livingston, a town 105 miles east of Nashville, came her native sons, among them congressmen, judges, business leaders and dwellers of the hills that border the town.

A great- nephew of Joseph and Ambrose Gore, soldiers of the American revolution, who for their valor under George Washington, received grants to the land on which the town now stands, sat on the speaker's stand, erected on the north side of the Livingston courthouse. Young Albert Gore, now of Carthage and superintendent of schools in Smith county was by right of descent ceded the honor of making the response to Mayor Charles J. Cullom's address of welcome at the exercises.

8,000 Attend Centennial

More than 8,000 persons thronged the square today to attend the centennial, and a continual flow of spectators drifted in and out of the big canvas tent erected over the speaker's stand. There was no set program watched by the majority of the crowd. There were hundreds of persons from Oakley, Monroe, Windle and Hilham., small towns nearby, who spent the day in Livingston with their families.

A.K. Lea of Livingston was chairman in charge of arrangements for the celebration, and introduced at the morning meeting, besides

Mayor Cullom and Mr. Gore, John Mitchell of Cookeville, attorney-general for the Fifth district: B. H. Hunt and C. C. Gore, Livingston Attorneys; Dr. Edward Clark, head of the public health departments in Overton, Pickett and Fentress counties, and Judge L. D. Bohanon, Overton county judge.

An accident in the audience, seated on long wooden planks before the stand, marred the exercise shortly after they had started. One of the planks gave way under the weight of the crowd, and splintered down on Mrs. Polly Livingston's leg, causing a double break just above the ankle, and slightly injuring Clara Kimes 11 daughter of Mr. and Mrs. Curtis Kimes.

On the speaker's stand was A. F. Eldridge 85 one of the oldest patriarches of the town and the son of Jess "Ranter" Eldridge, around whom centers the tale of the horse thieves and the manner in which Livingston became the county seat of Overton. According to the story "Ranter" Eldridge who wanted Livingston to be the county seat set out from Kettle creek now Clay county with several meighbors for Monroe where an election had been called to determine the county seat.

The party stopped for the night at an inn near Oakley 10 miles from Livingston. Early the next morning the irresponsible Ranter reputed to have been of the old school of Tennessee politicians arose with the dawn and chased off the horses of his neighbors who had come with him and who had intended voting against Livingston as the county seat. When the others arose they set up a great ____ and cry for their horses while Ranter went on to Monroe and voted. Livingston won the election by a margin of four votes.

A "Century of Progress" parade wound up the morning program and was taken part in by the American Legion and concert bands of Livingston and more than 100 paraders in costumes.

The parade was led by the bands, followed by two state highway motorcycle patrolmen and a group of small boys in costumes painted as Indians. Then came several covered wagons driven by muleteers dressed in the backwoods garb of the "long hunters" with fringed leather jackets and coonskin caps, who pioneered on the banks of Roaring River and settled Overton County.

A decorated float followed carrying a young girl dressed as an Indian maiden and women attired in the homespun aprons and big bonnets of early Tennessee vintage.

Emphasing the progress cycle came a float bearing students of the Livingston high school in modern dress representing the various departments of the school. A big red fire engine, modern in every detail brought up the rear of the parade.

Speakers on the afternoon program which began at 1 o'clock were Congressmen J. Ridley Mitchell, State Senator A. F. (Pat) Officer, speaker of the Senate Judge E. C. Snodgrass of Cookeville, of the state civil court of appeals, and Judge J. M. Gardenhire of Nashville.

All of the speakers were sons of Overton County and all of them in speaking indicated their pride in their nativity.

"The best Anglo-Saxon blood in the country," said Congressman Mitchell in his afternoon address flows in the veins of the people of this town whose sons have gone so far but who remain so true to the traditions of their youth.

Three baseball games were played at the close of the formal services in the afternoon and following a program of entertainment in old-fashioned square dance was held in the streets of the town tonight.

VISITORS CONVERGE ON LIVINGSTON AS STAGE IS SET FOR CENTURY OF PROGRESS CELEBRATION
(taken from Nashville Paper Aug. 1933)

Livingston, Tenn. Aug. 9 (Spl.)

Visitors from the four corners were converging in Livingston tonight; to attend the celebration Thursday of Livingston's 100 years of life.

Exercises will begin at 9 o'clock tomorrow morning marking a century of progress for this city which began on that eventful day when Jess Eldridge turned some horses out giving Livingston the opportunity to be voted the county seat of Overton County.

The city made final preparations tonight for the colorful event that is expected to draw thousands here Thursday for an anniversary celebration.

As the list of registrations grew tonight, families, friends and neighbors were making arrangements for reunions Thursday which are to be among the outstanding features of the greatest celebration this city has ever planned.

Among the early arrivals from distant points were Reuben Ray and family of Frederick Okla.; Will Keeton Myers and family of Tampa Fla., and Mrs. Minnie Lee Powell of Tampa.

On the program are a number of native Overton Countians some of them who now reside in other communities who will return to extoil the scenes of their childhood and praise its contribution to the state and nations progress during the past 100 years.

The list of speakers scheduled for addresses Thursday includes former Gov. A. H. Roberts now of Nashville; Atty. Gen. John A. Mitchell now in Cookeville; State Senator A. F. Officer, direct descendant of John Sevier; J. Ridley Mitchell member of Congress, Prof. Cornelious D. Judd of Denton, Tex., Gladstone H. White, now of Johnson City; George E. Lea now of Bradentown, Fla., and E. D. White, Ben H. Hunt, and Charles C. Gore, Livingston Attorneys.

Mayor Chas. J. Cullom will deliver the welcome and W. H. Hussey of Oklahoma will give the response.

Secretary of State Cordell Hull, who was born in this county has been invited to the celebration but may be unable to attend due to pressing official duties in Washington.

Bohannon Post No. 4 of the American Legion will stage the parade of progress the most colorful event of the community's greatest celebration. In charge of the parade will be N. H. Hankins.

Fiddling, dancing and comedy directed by Dr. W. M. Brown will be staged as features of the day's entertainment.

Early Settlement

The founding of Livingston began with the settlement of Ambrose and Joseph Gore, brothers who after serving their country in the Revolutionary war selected the site of the present town because of the spring they found in the wilderness here.

They built a house and the government gave them the land around this home as compensation for serving in the war. After settling on the place where the McAlpin home is now located the Gore brothers believing the site a good place for a town, sold 40 acres for a town site. The deed on record in the register's office shows that most of the markers and corners as set out in the deed were trees and it is believed that the plot was a wilderness at that time.

When Livingston was founded in 1833 Monroe was the county seat of Overton county. Livingston soon became a contender for the capital of the county and was selected as the county seat by a ruse conceived by Jess Eldridge.

Becomes County Seat

Eldridge setting out on horseback through a wilderness trail with six or eight of his neighbors for Monroe to vote on the proposed change of county seat spent the night before election somewhere near the place where Oakley is now located. Eldridge knowing his companions were determined to vote against the proposal arose early on the morning of the election and turned out the horses of his companions. Believing their horsed had been stolen the party began a search for the "thief" while Eldridge slipped into Monroe Livingston was selected by four votes.

Serving to make the gala event outstanding in the history of the county and its county seat are Alfred K. Lea, president Robert L. Eldridge secretary: Ben H. Hunt, Miss Allie Maynard, and Mrs. Pat Officer assistant secretaries, Millard H. Hankins, treasurer and Judge Le Bohanon, master of ceremonies.

Committees Serving

On the arrangements committee are Walter H. Boswell, Thomas R. Copeland, Dr. W. M. Brown, Dick Mitchell, Pat Officer, Lester Holman, Cato Taylor.

The invitation committee is composed of of Charles C. Gore, Frank T. Williams, Grover C. Peek, Robert A. Nunnally, Charles F. Lankford, Jack Dale and Dr. A. B. Qualls.

Finance committee: Charles D. Mitchell, Bedford Holman and William H. Estes.

Reception committee: James H. Myers, Allison Roberts, John Estes, John Hart, Dr. Doak Capps, Mack Smith and Arthur Ward.

Advisory committee: Sidney J. Bilbrey, Richard Hankins, Dr. Bill Breed, Phillip Myers, John A. Hargrove, Dr. L. F. Zachry, James W. Henson, Jim Lansden, K. L. French, John C. Bilbrey, Tom Brown, Lankin Maynard, Bedford Arnold, Cooper Deck, Ed Knight, Ernest Stockton, Berry Ledbetter, Maywood Copeland, Albert J. Mofield, Dr. Milton Qualls, Dr. Cecil H. Dowell, Brant Eubank, Sherlie Speck, John A. Miller, Marvin McCormack, Ras Poston, Alfred Keeton, Floyd Speck, Joe Almonrode, Thomas Bussell, Alex Smith and Hardin Winnigham.

MEMPHIS FEBRUARY 14TH, 1830
HELEN M' GREGOR STEAMBOAT DISASTER
ARTICLE PUBLISHED IN
ARKANSAS MORRILTON DEMOCRAT

FEBRUARY 20, 1830

IT HAS NEVER BEFORE FALLEN TO OUR LOT TO WITNESS AN EVENT OF SUCH A HEART RENDERING NATURE AS THAT WHICH OCCURRED AT OUR LANDING ON WEDNESDAY

MORNING. THE STEAMBOAT HELEN M'GREGOR, WITH ABOUT 410 PASSENGERS ON ABOARD, HAVING STOPPED AT THIS PLACE FOR A SHORT TIME, WAS IN THE ACT OF PUSHING OFF, WHEN ONE OF HER BOILERS HAVING BURST WITH A TREMENDOUS EXPLOSION, WAS THROWN FROM IT'S BED OVER THE FORECASTLE INTO THE RIVER: THE CHIMNEYS THROWN DOWN:

EVERY BOILER DISLODGED, AND THE BOILER DECK, ENGINEER'S ROOM AND ADJACENT OFFICES, MADE A COMPLETE WRECK IN AN INSTANT. TO GIVE AN ACCURATE DESCRIPTION ON THE SCENE WHICH FOLLOWED, WOULD EXCEED THE POWERS OF THOSE FAR MORE GIFTED THAN OURSELVES. A LARGE NUMBER OF THE DECK PASSENGERS, AS IS USUAL WHEN STARTING OUT OF PORT, HAD CROWDED TO THE FORWARD PART OF THE BOAT AND WERE ON THIS\ OCCASION THE PRINCIPAL SUFFERERS. AMID THE SMOKE AND DUST WERE TO BE SEEN, AT THE SAME MOMENT, THE DEATH STRUGGLE AND SPOUTING BLOOD OF THOSE WHO HAD RECEIVED THEIR MORTAL WOUNDS; WHILE THE SHRIEKS OF THE WOUNDED AND DYING WERE MINGLED WITH THE GENERAL CONFUSION. OUR CITIZENS RUSHED SPONTANEOUSLY TO THE SCENE OF THE DISASTER, AND BY THEIR ACTIVITY AND EXERTIONS RESCUED MANY A POOR FELLOW FROM A WATERY GRAVE. HOUSES WERE THROWN OPEN, OILS, LINTS, BANDAGES AND BLANKETS FREELY

FURNISHED FOR THE USE OF THE WOUNDED, AND SOME WERE SEEN EVEN CONTENDING FOR AND CLAIMING THE

RESPONSIBILITY OF NURSING AND PROTECTING SUCH AS THEY HAD BEEN INSTRUMENTAL IN SAVING. WE TAKE PARTICULAR PLEASURE IN NOTICING THE ACTIVITY OF OUR PHYSICIANS ON THIS OCCASION, ALL OF WHOM IMMEDIATELY REPAIRED TO THE SPOT, NOR CEASED THEIR LABORS UNTIL THE WOUNDED HAD RECEIVED EVERY ATTENTION AND COMFORT WHICH THEIR SITUATION REQUIRED. FOR THE SATISFACTION OF THOSE ABOARD, WHO HAVE MANY FRIEND AND RELATIONS ON BOARD OF THE BOAT, WE HAVE TAKEN THE PAINS TO COLLECT A LIST OF KILLED AND WOUNDED, WHICH WE ANNEX HERETO.

DOUBTLESS MANY WERE BLOWN OVERBOARD, WHO HAVE SUNK AMIDST THE WHIRLS AND SANDS OF THIS IMPETUOUS RIVER, NEVER TO RISE AGAIN. AS YET, HOWEVER, WE HAVE ONLY HEARD THE NAMES OF TWO WHO PERISHED IN THIS MANNER, WHOM WE HAVE INCLUDED IN THE LIST OF KILLED.

KILLED

RICHARD HANCOCK, LOUISVILLE, KENTUCKY
A. VAN METER, HARDIN COUNTY, TENNESSEE
? TALBOT, LONG REACH, OHIO
JAMES BLEDSOE, KENTUCKY
? CARROLL, CINCINNATI, OHIO
ED P. BEADLES, CLARK COUNTY, INDIANA
J. DUNN, EAST TENNESSEE
G.B. GILES, CINCINNATI
EPHRAIM GOBLE, BROOKVILLE, INDIANA
WILLIAM STOCKWELL, SALEM, INDIANA
DELANY, A FREE BLACK
ONE WHITE MAN, NAME UNKNOWN
WILLIAM EWING, CLARKE COUNTY, INDIANA
J. REAVES, HARRISON COUNTY, INDIANA

LEWIS YOUNG, A BLACK FIREMAN
A BLACK BOY, 12 TO 13 YEARS OLD

BADLY WOUNDED

GEORGE FREY, TIPTON COUNTY, TENNESSEE
JOHN CAMERON, CLARKE COUNTY, INDIANA
JOSHUA RICHARDSON, INDIANA
JOHN VALENTINE, MASS.
? DE HAVEN, PHILADELPHIA
JOHN LELAND, ONE OF THE PILOTS
J. SUGG, UNION COUNTY, KENTUCKY
? FILCHEN, UNKNOWN
Z. BAILEY OR BELL, HARDIN COUNTY, TENNESSEE
H. HELDRETH, MADISON COUNTY, INDIANA
JOHN ADDISON, ONE OF THE CREW
THOS. DRENARD, WILSON COUNTY, TENNESSEE
J. SWAN, LAWRENCE COUNTY, INDIANA
J.TENYCK, SHIPPINGPORT
WILLIAM CASE, NEW YORK
A BLACK MAN, NAME UNKNOWN

SLIGHTLY WOUNDED

? TYSON. CAPTAIN OF THE BOAT
? TURNER. ENGINEER
? GRAY, 2ND MATE
T.O'DANIEL, INDIANA
T.L. KNOWLAND, OHIO
J.MONASCO, TIPTON COUNTY, TENNESSEE
JOHN COONS, CLARKE COUNTY, INDIANA
WILLIAM POTTORFF
? DOHERTY, OVERTON COUNTY, TENNESSEE
THOS. BANK, LAWRENCE COUNTY, INDIANA
GREEN WILLIAMS, A BLACK FIREMAN

Miller Chapel Church made about 1938

March 1950 Miller Chapel Deed Service

The deed presentation service held at Miller Chapel Christian church Sunday afternoon March 19 was attended by approximately 125 persons from the community and from Dale Hollow Larger Parish. Following a brief historical sketch of the church building Bro. Bernard Taylor read the new deed to the property transferring the title from the Presbyterian Board of National Missions to the local congregation. He then presented it to Mr. Hassle McDonald chairman of the local church board who in turn spoke words of acceptance in behalf of the congregation. Edwin L. Becker Indianapolis Ind. brought the message of the day. Larger Parish pastors present were Curtis Holt Byrdstown George E. Miller Livingston, B. W. Covington Smyrna, Ewing S. Weakley and Bernard M. Taylor Alpine, and Vinton D. Bradshaw Wirmingham, Miss Connie Russell director of Christian education for Dale Hollow Larger Parish was also present. Churches represented by Layman present were McDonalds Chapel, Christ Church of Alpine, Livingston Christian, Smyrna Presbyterian, Bolestown Christian, Bethsaida and Midway. Vinton Bradshaw Pastor

Sam Brown home and family standing outside by fence this home was located and an article taken from 1933 newspaper states that in 1904 a storm from the west struck Windle the Store of W. J. Matthews was blown away and the home of Sam Brown blown down and his leg broken along with much timber down.

Windle Store built after storm destroyed other Matthews Store
building

The same article states that a storm struck the county in 1878
and in 1892. A heavy windstorm was very destructive to timber
at the head of Flatt Creek.

Article April 27, 1927

Exchange Club Notes

The local Exchange Club held their regular luncheon and meeting Tuesday night in the Masonic Hall.

A large number of members were present and several visitors, among whom, were: Mr. Harvey Winan a representative of the National Exchange club who made an inspiring talk on the activities of the club, also Mr. Wyatt Jacobs, of Vanderbilt University; Gladstone White; Prof Burgess, Thomas Copeland, of Livingston; John Davis, of Algood, and Messrs. Garrett, Clouse, Hicks, Whitiker, Allison, Hicks, Bilbrey, Officer, Sehon, Holloway, and Ray, of the Monterey Exchange club.

Mrs. Clair Walters and Miss Margery Copeland rendered a very pleasing musical program.

After the luncheon the club and visitors adjourned to the M. E. Church auditorium to hear Mr. Wyatt Jacobs of Vanderbilt University, and Mr. Gladstone White, a former student of Vanderbilt, debate a much discussed subject.

Resolved: That the 18th Amendment to the Federal Constitution should be repealed. Mr. Jacobs taking the affirmative and Mr. White the negative. The debate proved to be very interesting and after a heated argument the audience voted a negative decision.

Early community columns told much information years ago and even told of local deaths when no other obituary was written in local newspaper, so these articles are very informative and need to be read if researching family genealogy or history. The one that follows is a good example.

February 2, 1916
Willow Grove

Willie Patterson has been leading a class in vocal music at the Baptist church the past two weeks.

Lafayette Barksdale aged 83 died the 20th and buried in the cemetery Mr. Jim Smith conducting the funeral services. He leaves a wife and daughter, who have the sympathy of the entire community.

Cal. Willis of Bowling Green, Ky spent last week here with friends and looked after business matters.

Rev. Pete Bilyue of Cookeville has taken charge as pastor of the Baptist church and will preach the 4th Sunday in each month also Saturday night before.

The school here which has been in progress one month with Miss Edris Arms as teacher continues to grow in number of pupils and interest.

Dr. Sidwell has been very sick for several days but is again able to look after his patients.

Elmer Coulson and Orbor Overstreet are in Nashville.

Robt. Little of Livingston was here on Business last week.

Vann Watson has accepted a position as clerk for Coop Bros. at Peytonsburg, Ky.

Clay County Tennessee partially taken from Overton County some early history about it and some of the early post offices are included with this article.

Clay County Tennessee was established in 1870 and named in honor Henry Clay the county was taken from Jackson and Overton. Celina was selected as county seat. In a portion of Clay county that was taken from Overton county was a tract of 57,000 acres owned by John Sevier and which is mentioned in his some of his writings after his death in 1815 his widow moved to the Dale place known as the Clark later possibly.

Now with some information on part of the post offices that at one time were in Clay County or still are.

Celina: the county seat was taken from that portion of Jackson Co. and a post office was established with Robert B. Brown as the post master. It is still in operation in 1905 there were 228 living in the area there was flour and lumber mill, drug store, bank and several merchants in town.

Fox Springs: Daniel W. Cullom became post master in 1873 but the post office was discontinued in 1911 when it was moved to Oakley. In 1905, it had 10 people living there and J. C. Chowning ran the general store.

Lillydale: Had a post office from 1897 until 1943 when it was moved to Byrdstown. In 1905 there were 25 living in town with one general store Gamewell & Co.

Lime Springs: had a post office from 1877 but was discontinued in 1880.

Mount Pisgah: post office began here in 1870 was discontinued in 1878 this area was taken from Overton County.

Mouth of Wolf: land that was taken from Overton County a post office established in 1870 and continued until 1895 when name was changed to Lillydale and was located in what is now Pickett County.

Snakepoint: another small community with a post office from 1896 to 1908 when it was moved to Willow Grove no listing in 1905.

Speck: post office established in 1880 but was discontinued in 1911 when it was moved to Oakley. In 1905 there were but 11 persons living here with one general store run by A. M. Kimes.

<u>Sweet Gum Plains:</u> lasted only 18 months as a post office with two post masters James B Terry began 2 June 1873 and then Benjamin W. Stephens took over 5 September 1873 as post master this office was discontinued in December 1874.

<u>Willow Grove:</u> post office established here in 1876 but discontinued in 1942 when moved to Livingston. In 1905 there 18 persons calling this home and there was one flour mill and two general stores in the community.

Eastern Star To Have Banquet Saturday November 19, 1938

The members of the Livingston Chapter No 206 Order of the Eastern Star will h old a banquet in the Masonic hall at Livingston on Saturday nigh November 19th at 7:30 o'clock in honor of the oldest Masonic degree team in the State of Tennessee as well as in honor of all past Masters living or dead of Livingston Lodge NO 159 F. & A.M. which Lodge was organized in the year 1857 Eighty one years ago having had fifty three Masters up to and including the year 1937. The list designating the year each served as Masters the star indicates deceased as follows. *Hollen Denton served 1857,1858,1859 *Quinton D. Elder 1860 and 1865 * Dr. Henry M. Colquitt 1861 and 1866 *Carter A. Allison 1867,1868,1869,1870 and 1871 *C. C. Comee 1873 and 1874 * John S. Roberts 1875 * William P. Chaplin 1876, 1877 and 1881 * Thomas J. Cullom 1878, 1879, 1880 * Calvin E. Myers 1882, 1886, and 1889 * William A. Bicknell 1883, 1884 and 1887 * Alfred Lafayetts Windle 1885 and 1893 * Dr. Jacob M. Shelton 1888 * Moses Miller 1890 * J.K.P. Stewart 1891 * James H. Reed 1892 R. L. Mitchell Jr. 1894 *D. W. Martin 1895 *Columbus C. Carr 1896 *Dr. Melville B. Capps 1897 and 1898 John Hart Jr. 1900 and 1901 * William R. Officer 1899 * William O. Miller 1902,1904 and 1905 * John W. Allred 1903 Kennedy L. French 1906 L. D. Bohannon 1907 * J.A.M. White 1908 Thomas W. C. Carlock 1909 * Elmo C. Goodpasture 1910 William H. Estes 1911 Dr. William M. Breeding 1912 and 1916 Rev. John M. Brown 1913 John H. Estes 1914 Sidney J. Bilbrey 1915 William K. Draper 1917 John A. Miller 1918 *Jesse S. Fleming 1919 Waymon F.

Loller 1920 George O. Lea 1921 Luther P. Jernigan 1922 * D.D. Smith 1923 William T. Goff 1924 J. Grider Looper 1925 S. Baxter Smith 1926 William C. Smith 1927 Alfred K. Lea 1928 and 1937 Artie Hodges 1929 Cecil E. Rowe 1930 Charles A. Poindexter 1931 John Henry Salle 1932 Davis M. Smith 1933 Albert B. Smith1934 Carl H. Mofield 1935 Floyd W. Davis 1936. All past Masters all Masons all friends of past Masters and all who are friends of the Order are requested and expected to purchase a plate ticket which costs only fifty cents and attend. All past Masters are requested and expected to furnish a photograph size 8 X 10 or 10 X 12 inches to be displayed in the Lodge hall as the property of the Order to be preserved as such. The picture should be neatly and substantially framed and placed in the hall or in the hands of the committee not later than Friday November 18. In case of a deceased past master the relatives and friends are requested to provide a picture as described above. The arrangement committee asks that all tickets should be purchased not later than Friday November 18. The hall has a capacity sufficient to provide and care for 125 plates and persons. Miss Ruth Lee Mitchell past matron will be in charge of the sale of plate tickets and will be assisted by the Rainbow girls. Any information desired to tickets can be obtained from members of the committee composed of the following K.L. French chairman A.K. Lea and R. L. Mitchel The committee on refreshments is composed of Miss Udine Qualls, chairman Miss Rose Hart Dale Mrs. Mable Estes Mrs. Leila Belle Officer and Mrs. Eula Davis. Among the eminent speakers who are expected to attend are former governor Albert H. Roberts Congressman J. Ridley Mitchell Congressman Elect Albert Gore Past Grand Master A.K. Lea and Chancellor A.F. Officer of Livingston. Secretary of State Cordell Hull has been invited to attend Grand Secretary T. E. Doss and other Grand Officers are expected to attend.

K.L. French Chairman Alfred K. Lea R. L. Mitchell

May 22, 1834
William Wray Coroner of Overton County

Coroner's Sale

Pursuant to a writ of vendition exponas issued from the court of Pleas and Quarter session of Davidson county I shall offer for sale at the court house in Monroe, on Saturday the 12th day of July next, all right and title claim interest and demand that Hugh C. Armstrong has in and to the half of an undivided tract of land situated in the county of Overton on the waters of Nettle Carrier creek containing 30 acres more or less held by deed to said H. C. Armstrong and Ashby Dunegan levied on by two executions in favor of the bank of the state of Tennessee one against John Smelser, Valentine Mattock and the said Hugh C. Armstrong, the other against H. A. Bassett, Valentine Mattock and the said H. C. Armstrong, issued from the Davidson county court. Sale within the hours prescribed by law, unless debt and costs are previously paid.

July 1, 1938

Alpine Young People's Conference to be held July 4-9

The 14th annual conference of Presbyterian Young People of Cumberland Mountain Presbytery will open on the 4th of July, at Alpine. Rev. Eugene Smathers, Big Lick, chairman of the committee in charge of the conference, and Miss Alberta Burgess, also of Big Lick, president of the young peoples' group of the presbytery, expect to see a large group of young people at Alpine this year. The usual age of delegates is from 15 to 24 years, but others sometimes attend, especially adults interested in young people's work in the various churches. The teaching staff will be composed of Miss Janet Nute, of New York City "Youth at Worship" Dr. Julian P. Love "Techniques of Jesus;" Rev. Vernon Robinson "Essentiality"; Mrs. Flora Jones

"Highland Hermitage"; Rev. C. E. Cathey "Religious Drama and Pageantry"; Rev. W. G. Klein "Christian Youth Building a New Home"; Miss Ruth S. White "Our Presbyterian Church"; Rev. Paul McCormack "A Christian Feces Life Problems"; Rev. and Mrs. B. M. Taylor "Finding God in the Country"; and "Planning for Children in the local Church.

Delegates should arrive Monday afternoon, bringing sheets, pillow cases, towels and toilet articles (if planning to stay at the school dormitories); clothes and shoes suitable for recreation, musical instruments, and then have mail addressed in care of Y. P. Conference, Alpine. Bring a Bible notebooks texts pencils etc., can be bought at conference.

The cost per individual is $1 for registration. This will be all expense except a reasonable amount for text books, to those young folks who plan to stay at home or with friends. Young people boarding at the Institute will pay $4 additional. This is the most satisfactory arrangement and yields most benefit to the young person, usually, but local young people are invited and urged to attend also. The $4 board and room expense may be paid in produce as follows:

20lb Irish potatoes	$0.60
2lb bacon	0.30
6 doz. Apples	0.30
2 hens or 4 two-lb friers	1.20
5 lb string beans or 2 cans	0.25
3 qts. jelly or preserves	0.75
3 doz. Eggs	0.40
1 head cabbage	0.08
1 doz. Fresh cucumbers or green peppers	0.12
Total	Four Dollars

Come and help us to have a good conference.

The following are some pictures taken at Alpine area during the time period.

Mr. & Mrs. Taylor

Vespers with Dr. Love of Louisville KY & Mrs. Ruth White
music teacher

Vespers in shadow of the church

Children on a picnic day

Supper was always a picnic lunch

Picnic supper on table ready to receive sack supper

Group children attending conference

Leaving for home after conference

HISTORY OF BOY SCOUT IN OVERTON COUNTY
By A. M. Keeton February 1956

Troop I Boy Scouts of America was founded in the year 1914 in Livingston, Tenn. only four years after scouting was brought to USA by William D. Boyce, February 8, 1910, with eights boys in the troop. Bro. Sims now retired and living in Indiana was scoutmaster, with the following boys: Judge Pat Officer, Col. Harlan Taylor, Thurman Myers, Homer Stonecipher, Harry Mofield, Bob Smith, Jess Mitchell and Houston Roberts. The troop cabin was donated for a meeting place by Mr. Barnes and was about 3 miles from town. Sherley D. Bohanon became Scoutmaster, Thurman Myers Asst. Scoutmaster and Home Stonecipher as scribe. Headquarters in a cabin furnished by Judge Officer in the rear of his residence. From about the year of 1920 till about the year 1938, the records were all burned in a building owned by Prof. Garrett, who was Scoutmaster at that time. Troop 133

Boy Scout Troop 133 of Livingston was reorganized with the Lions Club as sponsor. Rev. W. C. Westenburger acted as Scoutmaster until he moved to Nashville. Then Rev. Hawkins of the Methodist Church took over the Scouts as Scoutmaster. Since then the Lions Club became inactive and the Methodist Church sponsored the Scouts after sometime the Scouts became inactive for about one year. Troop 133 was sponsored form 1941 to 1942 by Bohannon Post No. 4 American Legion, with the following committee; J. Q. McDonald committee chairman, C. C. Taylor, Cecil Dowell and A. M. Keeton, Herman Qualls, Scoutmaster and Romaine Billings assistant 1941 to 1942 with 22 scouts. Herman Qualls served as Scoutmaster 1942 to 1943 with 36 boys.

From 1943 to 1944 Troop 133 Scoutmaster, J. D. Eldridge, Robert D. Verble and Elmo Swallows, 30 boys in troop.

Ben Hawkins Scoutmaster 1944 to 1945 with 34 boys in troop. Hawkins resigned and Robert L. Oakley was Scoutmaster 1945 to 1946. Herman Qualls Asst. Scoutmaster, 41 boys in troop.

Herman Qualls Scoutmaster 1946 to 1947 with 41 boys in troop.

Raleigh Needham Scoutmaster from 1947 to 1955, then Eagle Scout Lowell Stephens was made Scoutmaster.

Overton County has only 3 Eagle Scouts to its records. They are Lowell Stephens, Floyd Jernigan and Clay Holman, Rev. Thomas Kern gained his Eagle Rank in Virginia. Lets all give the Cub Scouts a hand. The Cub Scouts has four packs.

CIRCUS HELD IN LIVINGSTON ON SQUARE
SEPTEMBER 22, 1856
Recounted by attendees in article September 28, 1927

A.L. Dale and A. C. Dale twin brothers attended the Robinson Bros. Great Circus Show in Livingston, Tenn. 71 years ago today, September 22, 1856. We lived on Obey's river sixteen miles from here. We rode horseback to Livingston the day before circus was to be and spent the night with J. D. Goodpasture an uncle of ours who lived on the square wher little Joe's café now stands. We went home that night after the circus was over. Respectfully yours A. L. Dale 87 years old.

FEBRUARY 1938 TRAGIC DUAL FOUGHT

The news of the startling duel Sheriff Alvin Carr and posse on one side and the Crabtree brothers on the other shocked this entire community Monday evening. The Sheriff and his posse found these young men at or near a wild cat still on the head of Mill Creek in the northern part of the County, when a pitched battle at once began. Tony Crabtree was killed. Wade Hampton Crabtree supposed to be wounded, escaped and James Crabtree was captured. The Sheriff had a states warrant for Tony for "wild catting" and Wade Hampton was wanted as a deserter from army service, he having refused to report for military duty. The officers found some bear tubs and were watching them when the three brothers came up. When ordered to surrender they opened fire with the above result. None of the officers were hurt, but several shots were fired at them. Another brother and the mother of these boys are her in jail on a charge of the theft of some hogs. James who was captured is about 17 y ears of age. The others are older. Later Wade Hampton Crabtree has surrendered to the Sheriff and will answer to Government demands as a soldier.

February 13, 1918 Article

SHERIFF KILLS TONY CRABTREE
Wade Crabtree a brother of Tony is wounded but escaped
Jim the other brother captured

Wade Crabtree, an outlaw of this county refused to obey the selective service law by filling questionnaire and notifying the sheriff of his intentions to resist arrest. It was generally understood that he was engaged in running and operating a wildcat still some four or five miles north of Livingston. ON Monday Feb. 11th the sheriff of Overton county A.J. Carr accompanied by his brother Billie Car, John Sebers a J.P. and his son Lester went into the locality of the Crabtree still. The officers hid themselves in the surrounding bluffs in the early morning and waited until some time in the afternoon when they discovered the approach of Wade Crabtree, accompanied by his two brothers, Jim and Tony. The Crabtree's were armed with double barreled shotguns loaded with number three buck shot, and judging from their actions they had been informed of the intended raid as they came over the hill they were looking in every directions with their guns loaded and socked. The sheriff waited until they were within thirty steps when he raised up and ordered halt, which was answered by a shot form Tony's gun which cut the brush in two or three feet of the sheriffs head he then rushed behind a tree and attempted to shoot the second time when the sheriff shot him in the temple with a Winchester the ball coming out through the back part of his head which resulted in death in a very few seconds while this taking place Jim Crabtree had dodged behind a barrel and laid his gun to the ground and was guarded by Billie Carr who was telling him all the time it he offered to raised his gun he would kill him, but in spite of his unfavorable surroundings he offered two or three times of raise his weapon. Wade the one the sheriff had orders from the government to arrest made his escape over the hill and as he was more familiar with the surrounding forest and as night was approaching he was not pursued by the officers.

NEW HITCHING GROUNDS FOR LIVINGSTON
January 1926

The town of Livingston has recently completed it's new hitching racks on the lot below the County jail. Accommodations have been made to hitch at least 250 horses. These racks have been built solely at the expense of the town and on the town's property and built for the convenience of the people form the country and it is hoped people will hitch there and not to fences and other places where the property of individuals will be damaged. Also it is hoped congestion in the streets and alleys on public days will be relieved. A few simple improvements such as this will eventually make a great difference in out town. Use the racks and not Private Property.

May 1928

CREMATED BODY OF WIFE NEAR BOMA

Posibly the most weird scene that was ever enacted in this section of Tennessee was staged one evening last week when John H. Nichols of Nashville brought the body of his wife who died in Nashville to an isolated spot near Boma in Putnam County and through the assistance of a kinsman John D. Nichols crudely improvised a cematory with logs and other timbers on which the body of the woman was placed after which the timbers were saturated with kerosene a match applied and the body consumed by the flames.

No one witness the weird scene or knew of its taking place except the two Nichols men who were carrying out the last request of the woman who had died of a dreaded malady form which she suffered for a long while. The obsequies were carried out exactly as she had planned them and the bereaved husband left the scene with a clear conscience of having done his duty as he saw it. The citizens of Boma were all but horrified when they learned of the action of the two men but on making inquiry were satisfied that their intentions were of the best and let the incident pass without further comment or criticism. It appears that there was a great deal of sentiment attached to the spot where the cremation took place by Mr. and Mrs. Nichols who many years ago spent their honeymoon there and had visited the spot in after years on camping trips which accounts for the strange request of the woman and subsequent carrying out of her plans by her husband. Putnam County Herald

ALPINE ACADEMY
September 1901

At the base of the famous Alpine mountains seven miles east of Livingston stands the somewhat aged building beneath whose roof hundreds of our most prominent citizens have received the mental and moral instructions that have made them a blessing to the country. Old Alpine was located on the summit of this classic mountain but the inaccessibility led to the removal of the location of the building to its present site. From the very first the school was crowded with phenomenal success until a few years ago when interest began to wane. At the last session of the McMinnville Presbytery arrangements were made to establish in a church training school in the bounds of the Presbytery and Alpine was selected as the best location. The school will therefore be under the joint control of a board of trustees appointed by __

Presbytery and the remainder board of trustees of the Academy. The ____ ____ under the new management will open on Monday the 30 inst. , with Prof. H. A. McCanley of Dyeersburg, Tennessee as

Principal. Assistants will be employed as needed. There is no better location for a school. Free from unhealthful and immoral influences and in the heart of a model intellectual, progressive, Christian settlement, it is a place no parent need have doubt about sending his child. The Enterprise is getting out the announcement for the coming year giving full particulars about board tuition etc. If you are contemplating sending a boy or girl to school write Prof. McCanley, Principal or L. H. Carlock Sec. Board Nettle Carrier, Tenn.

An Interesting Letter From A Former Overton Countian
Frederick, Okla. October 10, 1917

I wonder if we ever half realize when writing for the press how far and by how many of our old friends and acquaintances our letters may be read. Some four years past while I was sitting by the fireside of a friend in central Texas his wife was reading some news notes from either the Christian Messenger or the Christian Herald in which was the report of a number of graduates for Livingston Academy and to my great delight as well as surprise there appeared the names of two of my old school mates namely Miss Maude Hall and Paul Capps. Twas then I realized that though is old world may seem large with our modern way and __ments we are not far from each other. If you will spare me the space I want to tell of our experience since leaving Tennessee, yes Overton County in February 1901. We left Grandfather Bost's old home near Windle and came in wagon to Cookeville where we remained over night. Then and there begun some very memorable experiences to a boy of eight years and throughout that long week's journey I was a continual nuisance and worry to father and mother. I never sighted anything but that I wanted a more close survey of it and was always in danger by my curiosity. On Saturday afternoon about five o'clock we landed at our destination, the little town of Bonita Texas, where father met many boyhood friends among whom were the Howards, Langfords, Thomases, Flemings, Hollows, Bucks, etc.

The first year in Texas was a very miserable one for me. The sand blew all spring and I could not eat without gritting it in my teeth, (which complaint all new comers make but soon get used to it). People told us much about cyclones tornadoes and storms how awful they were and every time it thundered we made a buried dive for the "storm cave". We were told many stories about centipedes triangulars, reptiles, snakes, stinging lizards and scorpions of a thousand species, of how they had attacked people and that the sting or bite of each or any one meant sudden death. I was so scared that whole summer I would have run from a harmless junebug if I had seen one. I soon found that is by next summer that many of the stories were only imaginary and then I enjoyed life much as a bashful boy would. In the spring of 1910 mothers father J. H. Phillips (who was raised near Windle) who lived near this place came to Bonita to visit us. Mother returned home with him and stayed about a month and came home so full of Oklahoma fever that we all took it and could never quite get rid of it. So in October 1910 we hitched up our two old plug horses and loaded all our earthly belongings in the wagon and turned our course westward. Without any thing of very much importance happening we arrived in about a week at Grandfather Phillips home. Her too we met many Overton County men one of the first was Judge Hussey, whom father had known since boyhood and with whose children I had attended at Livingston. Some others we met were R. O. Ray, Steve Cooper, and some of the Hancocks and Copelands. I wonder now if any of my old time friends childhood friends remember me. In 1897 we lived on old Colonel's Hall place north west of Livingston in 1898-9 we lived on George Dillon's north farm up near the mountains and in 1910 we lived on Grandfather Bost's place near Windle. I must now close I fear very much that you can't give me space for as much as I have already written. But if this is published I may write again some time and tell you how we farm in Oklahoma. I love to read the Livingston news very much and also the news letters from nearby towns and places. Write often all of you.

I am sincerely

Wm. E. Bost

FATAL SHOOTING
November 26, 1916

News reached here Sunday night of the killing of Nathan Dale which occurred near the border of Clay and Jackson counties on Sunday afternoon. Dale was shot by a posse of revenue men in an auto mobile and died about two hours later. The full particulars of the unfortunate affair have not been ascertained siting many conflicting rumors as to the cause of the shooting have been going the rounds. Natha Dale was the son of Ans Dale a highly respected farmer of this county who lives near Henard. He was a married man and lived in Jackson county.

Livingston Route 2
November 26, 1916

Corn gathering is in full blast Corn is good

Mr. Eddie Richardson and Miss Georgia Dennis were married Sunday Rev. S. H. Flowers officiating.

Mrs. Martha Conner died Nov. 16th and was buried at the Cannon graveyard with the Rev. G. W. Burroughs conducting the funeral.

Mrs. Cora Hicks and children of Okla. have returned to the home of her father James Robbins.

Millard Conner wife and sister are spending a few days here.

M. V. Bilbrey and wife are visiting J. M. Conner's family at Willow Grove.

Mrs. H. C. Savage was taken to Nashville last week her husband and Dr. Sidwell accompanying her.

There was a spelling match at Lone Maple Saturday night. There was a lot of pistol shooting around I suppose they were celebrating the returns from Fentress county.

Vulean

New Era a McMinnville Newspaper Article 1868
Pertaining to Overton County TN

In Chancery at Livingston, Tenn.

March Rules, 1868.

H. B. Winningham, et als.
vs.   Bill to sell Land.
W. H. McDonald, et als.

IN this cause it appearing to the Clerk and Master from complainant's affidavit, filed in this cause, that defendants, the heirs of Weatley Smith, viz: Emmissa ———, formerly Emmissa Smith, and her husband, whose name is unknown, Emmalissa Smith, Minerva Smith, Logan Smith, and Emiline Smith are non-residents of the State, so the ordinary process cannot be served upon them; It is therefore ordered that publication be made for four consecutive weeks in the "New Era," a paper printed in McMinnville, requiring said defendants to enter their appearance herein and make defense to complainant's bill, at or before the next term of the Chancery court for Overton county, to be held at the courthouse in Livingston, Tennessee, on the 4th Monday in May, 1868, or the same will be taken for confessed and set for hearing *ex parte* as to them. J. W. WRIGHT, C. & M.

A. F. Caars, Sol. for compl't.   [mar12-1w

Early Chancery Court February 1868 at Livingston TN

In Chancery at Livingston, Tenn.
FEBRUARY RULES, 1868.
William Dennis,
    vs. } Orig. bill in nature of Cross bill.
The Tenn. and Cumberland Oil and Mining
    Company, et als.
    IN this cause it appearing to the Clerk and
Master from complainant's bill, which is sworn
to, that defendants, Charles Hequembour, Jr.,
W. C. Bunts, Secretary of said Company, and
Charles L. Hequembourg, Superintendent of
said Company, are non-residents of this State,
so the ordinary process cannot be served on
them, it is therefore ordered that publication be
made for four successive weeks in the NEW ERA,
a paper published in McMinnville, requiring said
defendants to appear at the next term of the
Chancery court for Overton county, to be held
in Livingston on the 4th Monday in May, 1868,
to plead, answer or demur to complainant's bill,
or the same will be taken for confessed and set
for hearing ex parte as to them.
    mar5-4   J. W. WRIGHT, C & M
J. D. GOODPASTURE, Sol. for compl't.

September 1898
Correspondence Monroe September 18, 1898

The health of this community is reasonably good at the present time. The farmers of this neighborhood made very good wheat this year. The corn crop looks very well except late corn which has suffered for rain badly. The pea crop is fine but a good rain would have helped. Some have sown oats and are preparing to sow another wheat crop. The news department is very scarce at this place now. But hope we will have more next time.

September 16 1898
From Hilham

Louis Christian and Miss Mollie Fleming were married on the 15th Dr. Langford officiating.

Mrs. Mollie Richardson, formerly Miss Mollie Mitchell died on the 15th at her home in Monroe county, Kentucky. She had been in poor health for quite awhile.

Pleas Buck and family and a Mr. Morgan left for Texas last Tuesday.

E. D. White one of Livingston's rising young lawyer's was here last Thursday on professional business.

Quite a wind storm passed over this vicinity last evening but no serious damage was done.

The saw mill, planer, grist mill and the spoke factory at this place are in full operation. Truly this town is business with a move on itself.

The traveling artist has been here this week.

September 12 1901
News Items
Booze (Special by Telephone)

Sept. 10 Mrs. J. L. Qualls died at her home near here last Thursday and was buried at the family graveyard. She had been afflicted for about two years.

A. W. Norrod is reported very low at his home near Hanging Limb. He has been sick for several weeks.

Several cases of scarlet fever are reported in this section but the disease is of a mild form.

NINETY OVERTON COUNTY BOYS GO TO C.C.C. CAMP
August 23 1935

Ninety one boys were accepted for membership in CCC camp and left on Wednesday for Camp Hill McAlister in Pickett County, according to an announcement given out today by Cecil E. Rowe administrator for Overton County. The list of boys who were accepted is a follows:

Tommie Norris, Grady Ferrill, Lester Eldridge, Robert Coleman, Hollie McCowan, Lee Brown, Jessie Freeman, Earl Gunter, Fred Winningham, Lanzie Winningham, Ezra Wilson, Edgar Garrett, Otto Crisp, Herman Copeland, Howard Bilbrey, Roy Ledbetter, Rudolph Flatt, Estes Burgess, Joe Grant Newberry, Othal Speck, Bethel Fletcher, William Honeycutt, Homer Key, Ernest Means, Lester Howard, Cleophus Key, Dewey Sisco, Cordell Ferrill, Cecil Speck, Mack Hammock, Milburn Ledbetter, Therman L. Key, Woodrow Hargis, Clarence Riddle, Willie Miller, Albert Lowhorn, Halton Holman, Elbert Greenwood, Delphus Dial, Charlie Carr, Fate Ledbetter, A. P. Ledford, Forrest Walker, Jewel Masters, Howard Norrod, Cassey Brown, Bob Pittman, Odel Walker, Frank Simcox, Marvin Sisco, Jerry McCowan, Burrice Howard, Ernest Hargis, Ulus Tucker, Carl Garrett, Robert Ray, Earl Spurlin, Dittle Smith, Lonnie Ledbetter, Harvey Garrett, Albert Copeland, Lidge White, Leabort Johnson, Carlon Dishman, Horace Sams, Troy Ford, Charles Little, Price Hargis, Ralph Smith, Hobert Peyton, Ralph Conner, Willard McGinnis, Curtiss Lee Johnson, Stanley Hall, Hayden Deck, Clifford Robbins, Carvel G. Tayse, Vernon Almonrode, Horace Norrod, M. C. Wells, Marshall Ledford, J.D. Daniels, Dallas Wilson, Ridley Byers, Frank Kirby, Ernest Neal, Richard Winningham, Herbert J. Smith, Carl Neal, John Armas and Malcom Robbins.

Odds and Ends Of History
By A. R. Hogue Author
Collector Historical Material

EARLY SETTLERS IN OVERTON
NOW FENTRESS COUNTY

The Bible says "Honor thy father and thy mother that thy days may be long in the land which the Lord thy God giveth thee" I can think of no way in which we can honor our parents that is better than collecting and recording facts about them and their lives. In my way of thinking this beats a crumbling stone monument.

The first settlers in Fentress County were in the Wolf River Valley the first settlers lived near the Three Forks of Wolf River. It was then supposed to be in Cumberland County, Ky. In 1798 the families of Huddleston and of Winningham are known to have lived there through court records involving title to the land. This part of Fentress County became Overton County eight years afterward, and Fentress County in 1823. The deed records show that Adam and George Helms lived on Wolf River near where Forbus is now located in 1807. Conrad Pile, great-great-grandfather of Sgt. Alvin C. York, became a resident of this region about 1801. Valentine Hatfield lived on the Middle Fork of Wolf River in 1820. William Hinds a son of Levi Hinds lived on Wolf River in 1821. John Riley an ancestor of the Riley family in Fentress County lived on Caney Creek Wolf River in 1824. Thomas Huckeby lived near Black House on the head waters of Wolf River in 1825. Joshua Storie, , Samuel Poor, Robert Storie, Bessy Young and Ephraim Hatfield lived on Wolf River in 1826. Neely Grooms lived near the David Ross tract on Wolf River in 1827. Arthur and Strother Frogge lived on Wolf River in 1820. The names of all these settlers appear in early deed records in Overton County.

Other early settlers too numerous to mention are omitted.

Early grants covering the section were issued by North Carolina to Stockly Donelson and John Sevier. Both these grants were issued prior to 1796 when Tennessee became a state. These grants covered lands now lying in both Overton and Fentress.

Some early settlers in other communities will be furnished in a future article.

I am often asked how I get the facts given in "Odds and Ends". The answer to this query is I have spent years in collecting historical information through old books, old papers, and some of it has come from conversations with people old and young.

A part of this information I have published in book form. The material in these books was collected and compiled in spare time through the past 40 years. My first book was published in 1914.

The names of many early settlers may be seen in Mark Twain's Obedstown now on sale by Upper Cumberland Times.

Every tombstone preserves history. The graves we see contain buried history that is lost forever through our neglect to talk with those who lie buried there and to preserve their recollections about their lives and the lives of their ancestors while they lived and walked among us.

A. R. Hogue

**Overton County Sheriffs Department 1968
L-R Vanis Hawkins, James Eldridge Sheriff, Carson
Winningham, John Hawkins, In back L-R Jess
Greenwood,Lewis Newberry, Hoyt Deck**

PATTERSON WAS THP OFFICER ASSIGNED TO OVERTON COUNTY IN 1968
History of Overton County
Special article July 1930

Overton county lies in the north central part of the state is bounded on the north by clay and pickett counties on the east by fentress on the south by Putnam and Jackson. The county contains 277,312 acres. The drainage of the county is all towards Cumberland river which lies a few miles beyond the western boundary. Governor John Sevier located two grants for over 57,000 acres of land for Overton county, now Overton and Clay counties. A permanent settlement in the area was established at Hilham in the 1800, two other settlements were made near the present site of Livingston before this time. As early as 1770 the region had been occupied by hunters for sometime but there was no permanent settlement. In 1806 the county was organized by the following pioneers Adam Gardenshire, Adam Deck, Abraham Goodpasture, Isaac Gore, Jacob Swallows, Joseph Copeland, Moses Fiske, Aaron Pitts and John Eldridge. The county seat was established at Monroe in 1810 where it remained until 1835 when it was removed to Livingston the present county seat.

In 1842 Putnam county was organized and a part of Overton County was added to that county. In 1870 Clay County was organized and a part of Overton added to Clay also Pickett which was organized in 1879. Overton county was named for Judge John Overton Judge Overton was a friend of Gen. Andrew Jackson the president and bought two tracts of land in this county from Jackson.

Historical Spots

The old Hickey place located in the 7th district was the scene of the first courts of the county. In the 3rd district south of Hilham the first Jackson county courts were held. A beautiful spot and with a historical background is the old Zollicoffer battle of Mill Springs in 1861, Camp Springs where Gen. Felix Zollicoffer camped with his troops just before the Myers located in the 11th district was where Capt. Luther Myers camped with his troops on their way to Mill Springs, Pilot Knob overlooking Monroe, Tennessee, also the Beard Mountains near Allons, were used as signal stations during and after the war. Robert Crockett was killed on Matthews creek about 1817 and is buried near oak hill. Alpine is the site of the old Alpine Academy. Hilham is the site of the old Fiske Female Academy. Monroe is the site of the first county seat.

Great Men

Overton County's great men art is glory and pride. Its sons have filled with distinction every profession and avocation of life. Among the distinguished physicians are doctor Henry Colquit, Simon Hinds, B. J. Bledsoe, John B. McDonald and B. D. Simms. Some of the noted teachers are Doctors Moses Fiske, Rev. B. W. McDonald D.D., John I. D. Hinds. Some of the noted preachers of our country of our county are Elder Wm. A. Potter who began to ride this circuit in 1829. There was over 100 miles in his circuit at that time. John W. Phillips, L. P. Holsom, Harris and Dennis of the Methodist church the Reverends John Landsden. A. H. Goodpasture, T. W. Pendergrass, John Hinds and T. F. Bates of the Presbyterian church, Elders Caleb Sewell, Isaac T. Reneau and Rev. Chilton of the Christian church.

Overton county has still been more honored in its legal profession. Among the first lawyers are Adam Huntsman, Jacob Dillen, Stockley B. Raven, Jas. B. Gardenhire, Daniel McMillin, Judge Edward Cross,

Judge E. L. Gardenhire, Judge W. W. Goodpasture, Judge R. S. Windle, James W. McHenry, Judge William Cullom, Attorney General James W. Wright, General John M. D. Mitchell, Samuel Turney, James A. Whiteside, Judge R. Nelson.

The only governor Overton county has supplied to date is Governor A. H. Roberts, who was born and reared in Overton county was educated at the Alpine Academy was later county superintendent of public Intsructions of Overton county, was Chancellor of the fourth Chancery Division serving nine years when he resigned this office and was elected Governor of Tennessee. Some prominent statesmen of Overton county were Judge W. W. Goodpasture who became Judge of his county was born and reared near Hilham received his education at Alpine was admitted to the bar when quite young. Others are Hon. William Cullom, Hon. E. L. Gardenhire, Hon. John L. Beverage and Jefferson Dillard Goodpasture.

Products

Livingston, Tennessee Overton County ranks second as a poultry market in the state. In 1927 there were 50 car loads of poultry shipped from Livingston. Our forest products seem unlimited. We have cedar, walnut, oak, dogwood, maple and popular. More golf sticks are made and shipped from Overton county than any other county in the state. There are now ten million feet of lumber in Livingston ready to be shipped valued at a half million dollars. The principal crops grown in this county are corn, wheat oats and hay, sorgum, Irish potatoes and sweet potatoes, the estimated value of our livestock for 1927 was six hundred fifty two thousand, and three hundred and twenty two thousand.

Overton county is peculiarly rich in architectural stones which harden on with the age. Petroleum natural gas and coal are each obtained in Overton county. As a source of lime Overton county could supply the world for several centuries. Overton coal mines and Brier Hill Colleries are located in Overton county, form which a vast amount of coal is shipped annually.

Education

The first schools of any importance established in Overton County were the Fiske Academy at Hilham and the Alpine Academy at Alpine, Tenn. The Fiske school was the first distinctive female school chartered in the South and one of the first in America. It was founded by Moses Fiske in 1823. The Alpine school was founded by John Dillard in the same year. One of the oldest teachers of this school was Professor Davis, Governor Beverage of Illinois was also a teacher in this school.

Professor Bowden father of Mrs. A. H. Roberts wife of ex-Governor Roberts taught there. Several prominent men of our county received their education at Alpine among them Hon. A. H. Roberts, Congressman Sprouls of Nebraska, Senator Shelby M. Cullom, who became Governor of Illinois.

It is said the first Tennessee history taught in the state was taught here to a class of 80 who that year each had a school in the state of his own, and taught this history. This school is now a mission, under control of the Board of Presbyterian church. It is a thoroughly equipped four year high school.

Overton county has four two year high schools of which the Livingston Academy is the largest. This is a mission school under the control of the United Missions of the Christian church. They have both boys and girls dormitory and modern brick high school building thoroughly equipped.

Overton county has 115 teachers aside from those at Livingston and Alpine. The schools are now running a full eight months term as required by the state. There are three junior high schools located at Hilham, Rickman and Crawford.

Prof. Jim Champlain one of the founders of the Blind School at Nashville, was a citizen and teacher in Overton county.

Overton county has one missionary in Japan, one who has seen services in Mexico and one who is ready to go to India, when the Board will send her.

War History

In the War of 1812 our records show two Overton countians, Lieut. William Burrus and Major Jonathan Burrus.

This was the home of Capt. C. E. Myers the last surviving Tennessean of the Mexican War and other Mexican soldiers were Burris Martin and Richard Copeland.

Civil War Capt. C. E. Myers organized our first company of soldiers May 8th, 1861, the name was the Overton county guards. Other Captains were Jas. McHenry, Luther Myers, W. W. Windle, W. H. Fleming, Jim McHenry, John S. Roberts, Joe Bilbrey, Richardson Copeland, Sam Davis, H. B. McGinnis. Overton county had one Colonel, John H. Hughes, one Major W. P. Chapin, one Lieutenant Colonel F. H. Daugherty and twelve Lieut., as follows Loyd Chapin, Fay Goodbar, Felix G. Bilbrey, A. L. Dale, Fayette Windle, J. R. Donaldson, Jeff Bilbrey, Robert Parker, Tom Webb and I. Horner.

We had 625 men on record in the World War and lost 41 men, some killed in action and others died of disease. Overton county was represented in the World War by practically two volunteer companies officered by one Major Burks, one by Capt. Stephens, three Lieut. Shirley Bohannon, John A. Mitchell and M. M. Roberts, one Sergeant E. L. Norrod. This county had more men according to population in World War than any other county in the Tennessee, and possibly more casualties.

This county was represented by 8 men in the Spanish American War.

RAGLAND-POTTER COMPANY
Livingston, Tennessee

July 1930

The Ragland-Potter Company wholesale grocers as organized in 1915 at Murfreesboro, Tenn. with one store. From this small beginning in the fifteen years of its existence, Ragland-Potter Company have grown rapidly. They now operate eight stores located as follows: Manchester, Chattanooga, Lebanon, Watertown, McMinnville, Sparta, Cookeville and Livingston. They still have the main office at Murfreesboro, Tenn.

The Ragland-Potter store at Livingston, Tenn. is located in the wholesale district in the old Maxwell-Hill Company building. This building has been renovated inside and out and is now a modern up to date plant. The Ragland-Potter Company began business here in September 1925. Since that time their business has steadily grown, till at present they supply a large part of this upper Cumberland country with their products. Their trucks are constantly traveling the highways, loaded to the guard, delivering their goods to communities that cannot be reached by railroads.

Ragland-Potter Company of Livingston, Tenn. has a fine corps of workers, giving efficient service and are always courteous to their customers. They carry a complete stock in their line, and the best the market affords at a reasonable price.

BEAUTY SPOTS IN OVERTON COUNTY
July 1930

Zollicoffer Springs is a beautiful spot located about two miles from Livingston on the road to Hilham. This spring was named in honor of Felix K. Zollicoffer, who made camp there and trained his soldiers before the battle of Cumberland Gap. The tall stately forest trees the grassy glade and cool sparkling water make this and ideal camping place. The Woman's Civic Club hopes to place a marker on this spot soon. The York Highway now under construction leads by this beautiful spring.

Along the banks of the Old Roaring River is an ideal fishing and camping ground. The river winds through a lovely valley of wild beauty and the banks along its courses are lined with forest trees over a century old. Many lovely springs afford ideal camping places. There are several old mills located throughout the county on its many water courses that for natural beauty are equal to any in the United States. Among them are Garrett's mill, Matthews mill, Crawfords mill. The Highways of Overton county lead through scenery equal to any in the United States. They wind through the mountains affording views of far flung valleys or surpassing beauty. Many tourists have exclaimed over the beauty along the highway of Overton County.

A Tribute To Livingston
August 1933 written by a former Overton County resident

Dear, dear old Livingston
My childhood home so sweet
I love each flower, tree and stone
And Friend upon your street

Today how I'd like to be there
Your birth to celebrate
But ah, I'm far from your land so fair
For such has been my fate

Oft times in fancy on gipsy wheels
I wander back to pleasant streams
And thru mem'ry's vista my heart feels
The yesteryears brighten my dreams

Say 'hello' for me to my friends old town
For you are still sweet home to me
And as they give you a laurel crown
I'll think of you longingly

Goodhope school house so tiny made
It stood on a corner of the home farm
Lessons done in its shade we played
The place for still holds its charm

Life's pathway sometimes has seemed so long
Since I sadly said goodbye old Friend
But in my heart I have kept your song
Sweet remembrance and cheer I send

What great things have been done in thy day
Wonderful deeds and the splendid roads
And all who travel along your way
Will find you've helped to lighten their loads

Can't your hear sweet music echo of your band
Heartsongs of the Pioneers on the golden shore
If they view what you've wrought in town and land
They wish you another century and more!

Mrs. M. O. Ward

Nee Sallie Roberts
Modesta, California

Served in House of Representatives and State Senate

William J. Matthews Jr. was born 18 July 1861 and died 19 November 1951 at the age of 90 called "Uncle Bill" by friends. He was from Windle community in Overton County. W. J. served in House of Representatives of TN 50th General Assembly 1897, 51st 1899, 58th 1913, 59th 1915 and 67th 1931 and a member of State Senate 60th General Assembly 1917, and 61st 1919, as a southern democrat a party that he was proud of. He owned a store at Windle ran the post office for 19 years received his 50 year service in 1945 from the Free and Accepted Masons Lodge No. 259 Livingston, statistical correspondent of Overton County for the Department of Agriculture. He not only owned farms in Overton County also in Oklahoma and Texas. He served the county with pride telling stories of the settlers of the county till his death. W. J. Matthews Jr. and wife Mary F. Webb had 13 children several descendants still live in the county and are proud to descend from this family.

Fred Wright General Merchandise Store

This store was located at Wirmingham Community in Overton County TN large crowd on porch and standing out in front of store.

J. M. Wright Building at Wirmingham

Fred Wright standing in doorway of large double doors this not only housed General merchandise store also the post office was located here as well. In front at the top in the center of building it has J.M. Wright building

Rebecca (Flowers) Wright and neighbor hanking thread outside many years ago.

Rebecca and neighbor finishing up with thread looks like now will it be ready for them to use.

OVERTON COUNTY ERECTED IN 1806
BY ACT OF LEGISLATURE OF TENNESSEE
First settlers came from Virginia,
North Carolina and Kentucky

By Robert L. Eldridge

Overton County is located in the north-eastern section of Middle Tennessee it was erected by an Act of Tennessee Legislature on September 12, 1806 the area coming from a part of Jackson County and from the Indian reservation known as "The Wilderness". As originally planned Overton County embraced besides its present limits all of what is Pickett and Fentress counties parts of Clay, Putnam, Cumberland, Macon and Scott counties.

The first known visit to this county was made in 1769 by a party of three hunters, Kasper Mansker, Joseph Drake, and Robert Crockett who established a camp near the present site of Oak Hill in the 5th District where they spent some time collecting furs. Their camp was attacked by the Cherokee Indians and Crockett was killed he was the first of his race to die in Middle Tennessee.

Drake and Mansker returned to their homes in Stockton Valley KY and were so impressed with the country that they gave such glowing accounts of the section that other hunters made their way over the mountains looking for suitable places to make their home. To them it was an excellent country a land of freedom plenty of game and fertile soil with fine water and abundance of fine timber ideal climate and but few signs of the Indians.

The majority of the early settlers came from Virginia, North Carolina, Kentucky and East Tennessee. They came for various reasons many came as hunters and adventures but perhaps the outstanding thing that attracted their attention was the fact that they could get plenty of land cheaply much of which they bought with land warrants issued by the State of North Carolina for services in the Revolutionary War.

First Unknown

Perhaps the first permanent settler is not known but various claims have been made by different families that their ancestors were among the early settlers among which are Copeland, Goodpasture, Captain William Watson, Captain Jesse Arnold, Totten, Sevier, Eldridge, Bilbrey, Fisks, Allen, Mitchell, Langford, Hinds, McDonald, Irons, Windle, Matthews and many other families were pioneer settlers.

The ninth section of the act creating the county provided that the courts of said county should be held at the home of Benjamin Totten who was the first county court clerk, Valentine Matlock first sheriff, James Turney the first circuit court clerk and James Taylor, Wm. Evans, Isaac Oakes, John Reagan, John Coonz, Abel Willis, James Turney, Francis McConnell, Robt. Mitchell, Squire Poteet, Samuel Brown, Peter Williams, Allen McDonald, George Armstrong, John Taylor and Henry Rayburn who were the commissioned on 20 April 1807 were there first Justices of the Peace. A military department was organized and the officers commissioned on 13 May 1807 with Lieutenant Colonel Stephen Copeland commander of the county. Hilham the oldest town was laid off in 1805 by Moses Fiske through whose efforts Fiske Female College was established at that place by an act of the Legislature 11 September 1806 to which institution Fiske and Sampson Williams contributed one thousand acres of land.

Monroe County Seat

Monroe was made the county seat in 1810 it was this place that Geo. Willis opened the first store in the county in 1809 the majority of his merchandise being hauled from Baltimore, MD in wagons. Monroe soon became a thriving little town a court house and jail were erected criminals were placed in stocks sent to the whipping post and branded with hot irons as punishment for crimes.

The post office was established at this place in 1823 settlers located near Alpine at an early date near this place the Cherokee Indians formerly had a village with Nettle Carrier as Chief. A Cumberland Presbyterian Church was organized here by the pioneers and was perhaps the first in the county. John L. Dillard erected a log school house here in 1846 and in that fall his son Wm. M. Dillard began teaching. This school known as Alpine Institute had a rapid growth and soon became a popular school in which many students received a classical education and became prominent in state and national affairs. Gov. A. H. Roberts was principal of this school some time after the War Between the States.

Livingston was founded in 10 August 1833 when Joseph and Ambrose Gore deeded 40 acres of land to the commissioners for the town of Livingston by and act of legislature the county seat was moved from Monroe to Livingston in 1835.

Each decade in the history of the county forms a fascination chapter within itself as changing manners and customs make their imprints as the courageous builders of a great county.

THE AMERICAN LEGION AUXILIARY

The American Legion Auxiliary of Bohannon Post No. 4 Livingston Tennessee was organized 17 March 1930 under the direction of Mrs. Donna Falker state vice-president with twenty-four charter members with officers as follows.

Miss Geneva Bohannon Unit President, Mrs. A. F. Officer Unit Secretary, Mrs. J. B. Fleming Unit Treasure. Since the organization there have been nine member added making a total of 33 with seven Gold Star members.

It is the aim and purpose of the Auxiliary to cooperate with the Legion to erect a memorial in honor of the Overton County Soldiers also to assist in rehabilitation work throughout the state. Those eligible for membership in the Auxiliary are the wives, mothers, sisters and daughters of members in good standing in some Legion Post in Tennessee also relatives of soldiers who died in service.

INTEREST IN OIL DRILLING GROWING
IN THIS SECTION
July 1952

Much activity has recently been manifest in the oil business in Overton County with several wells in operation and in the process of being drilled. Most of the activity centers on and near the Capps property downstream on Roaring River. Dr. J. D. Capps was in Kentucky last week in the interest of his oil operations. The Capps No. 2 well is now down to 100 feet and work is progressing according to schedule. Dr. Capps and his associates will begin No. 1 on the Vester Geesling farm the first of next week. Mr. Greenup another oil operator has three wells drilling on Roaring River downstream from the Capps lease. He has three wells on pump making 300 barrels a day. A Kentucky company is drilling on the Booze Garrett farm near Timothy. A Michigan company is drilling on the Buford place near Rickman. Excitement is running high over these wells prospects. Overton County is at last in for a test.

CEDAR LAKE CAMP TO OPEN SUNDAY 15 JUNE 1952

Cedar Lake Camp for boys and girls ages 8 to 15 opens its 11th season 15th June. The camp located five miles east of Livingston is directed by its founders Rev. and Mrs. Henry C. Geiger. Bro. Geiger is also director of the Children's Gospel Hour which is broadcast each week over 91 stations and heard in Livingston every Saturday morning on station WHUB at 9 o'clock. The boys camp is from June 15 to 20 and the girls come June 29 to July 13. Though the program for both camps is geared for the full two weeks period campers may enroll for one week. The purpose of the camp is to give boys and girls a vacation of fun and recreation to develop physical skills and to provide for their spiritual needs. Cedar Lake is distinctively a Christian camp. The recreation includes swimming under qualified supervision, softball, shuffleboard, badminton, archery, volleyball and other sports. The camper may try his hand at woodworking in the supervised workshop or at pottery, felt craft and other handicrafts.

The daily menus include milk meat and fresh vegetables prepared by excellent cooks. Write to Cedar Lake Camp Livingston Tenn., for camp folder and complete information.

Early Post Card advertising Cedar Lake Camp

INDEPENDENCE COMMUNITY SALUTES
MR. AND MRS. JAMES W. MARTIN
Article 2 December 1949

Mr. James W. Martin better known as "Uncle Jim" was 95 years old Nov. 11 of this year. He has lived his entire life within the borders of the Independence community was educated, married, raised and educated his family within the community. Mrs. Martin the former Callie Waddell was born in Kentucky August 25 1870 but moved to Tennessee at the age of six to a farm in the nearby Ozone community. She married James W. Martin 60 years ago February 13 1889. To this union was born 9 children 3 of whom are still living. They now have 17 grandchildren and 8 great grandchildren. Mrs. Martin has been a member of the Church of Christ for 30 years. The Martin home near the Oakley division of the community is a large two story white house which they built themselves and moved into in 1919. They live alone now but their home has been modernized recently with the installation of a new and complete bathroom, hot and cold running water and is serviced with electricity. It is easy to identify the Martin home by the large beautiful cedar grove on the right of the house. It has been revealed that this was once the site of an apple orchard but in 1851 a storm twister blew down the entire orchard in the following spring it was discovered that hundreds of little cedar seedlings had come up in the area, they were left to grow and today it is one of the finest cedar groves in this country. They have had many large offers to buy the timber but have steadily refused to sell. Mrs. Martin insists it is a wonderful windbreak and that it is worth more to them standing as it is. Mr. Martin chose farming as his occupation general rather that specialized farming. Mrs. Martin says that all her talents were directed toward homemaking. They have been acquainted with war Mr. Martin's brother served in the Confederate Army during the Civil War they had two sons in World War I and two grandsons in World War II. They Martins have seen many changes take place in the community within their lifetime. They enjoy good health and live alone at present but their home is a favorite gathering place neighbors and relatives. Independence community salutes Mr. and Mrs. Martin its oldest residents.

Overton Woman Marries Farmer Who Ran Wife Ad
Couple are married in County Court Clerks Office
by Rev. S. D. Organ
IT PAYS TO ADVERTISE
Article 11 September 1936

Willie Benson 35 Flintville farmer who advertised for a wife and planned to get married July fourth only to have his plans disrupted was married Labor Day but to a different woman. Benson's advertisement for a wife appeared in the weekly newspaper of his home county, Lincoln County and also in the Nashville Banner. The report was broadcast by the Nashville Banner News hawk. Later a young woman wrote him and plans were made for a wedding but the girl's father objected as she was under age. In the meantime Miss Rosa Nivens daughter of Joe P. Nivens respected farmer of the Mt. Gilead community, Overton County saw the newspaper notice and it resulted in the two being brought together for the first time four weeks ago. The announcement followed and the wedding ceremony was performed Monday in the office of County Court Clerk H. E. Swallows with the Rev. S. D. Organ pastor of the Methodist Episcopal Church south officiating. Miss Minnie Nivens sister of the bride was bridesmaid and Thomas J. Steward was best man. After the wedding Mr. and Mrs. Benson returned to Flintville to live. Mr. Benson said he received many answers to his advertisement which read "Wife wanted age 17 to __ unable to read the other age. At once for I need some one as my mother is dead and left some property that I want to make over to any one desiring to marry a nice young man."

Article 11 September 1936
MAN CHEATS DEATH AFTER FALLING TO SLEEP ON RR TRACK
Escapes with minor injuries when thrown from track by cowcatcher returning from dance.

Cookeville- Lester Hicks 25 former WPA worker is recovering from numerous cuts and bruises and a broken arm received when he was struck by a west bound Tennessee Central freight train at Algood about 4 o'clock Sunday morning when he sat down on a rail to rest and fell asleep. Hicks said that he had been to a dance at Rickman Saturday night and was tired and sleepy when stopped near the Algood station to rest a few minutes. Dr. J. T. Moore Algood physician who arrived at the scene a few minutes after the accident said the engineer of the train stated that he saw the man sitting on the rail and blew the whistle several times to warn him of his danger. Obviously failing to hear the whistle and remaining on the track. Hicks was struck by the cowcatcher of the locomotive and thrown about six feet into a ditch. Dr. Moore stated and said he could detect no signs of drunkenness on the part of the victim. The injured man is the son of Mr. and Mrs. M. C. Hicks of Cookeville.

Rainbow Falls located in Alpine community area
27 April 1942

Rainbow Falls at the base

LEE AND GILBERT SCHOOLS AT ALPINE
REMEMBERED BY A. G. NORROD
Article 17 February 1950

Since the people at Alpine are collecting information for a history of their community and since they are building a memorial to contain a museum as well as a library and a post office. I thought I would write down some of the things I remember about my school days in Alpine.

The next school after the Davis School was taught by O. E. Lee from March 12 to July 12 1883. This school was taught in the building erected by Prof. Davis and later occupied by the Bowden-Roberts school. The following attended the Lee school.

Belle McDonald daughter of Ewing and granddaughter of Dr. John McDonald who lived here at the foot of Alpine mountain. Belle's mother Selina was a Woods and came from Kentucky. Ewing died and she being a widow married Dr. Henry Stephens who was a medical doctor and a preacher and the greatest orator I ever heard. He was a good doctor too when Andy Franklin was a boy Dr. Stephens treated him for malaria and chills.

Belle married a Dalton in Kentucky. Mrs. Winnie McDonald is a friend of hers. Viola McDonald sister of Belle, Viola married Lee Fitzgerald died in New Mexico. Allison sisters daughters of Squire J. B. Allison Flora who married Will Winton was the mother of Mrs. Pearl Brown and Mrs. John O. Smith, Mollie married a widower, Harve Peters at Clarkrange, Ova who later taught school at Alpine married John Bowden and lives in Crossville.

In talking with Andy Franklin I find he attended two of Miss Ova's schools. Ledbetter sisters daughters of Mack Ledbetter who lived in the place that later belonged to Frank Smith brother of John then to Berry Jones and now to Johnnie B. McDonald. Dady married Jim Teeples and their daughter married Mr. Scott a merchant and timber man. I believe Old Jim Teeples, now blind, lives with them.

Tiney. Winton sister's half sisters of Hutson and Ridley Mullins. Florence she died of TB and is buried at Goodhope. Eta married Will

Smith who died later she married Lansden Robbins who taught school at Alpine. He died too, she now lives in Berea, KY.

Lizzie Smith daughter of Jim Smith and sister of John married Foster Winton and lives at Alpine. Sallie Jackson daughter of Sutton Jackson married a widower Squire Bilbrey and so was Mr. Sid Bilbrey's step-mother.

Winnie Jackson daughter of Preacher Josiah Jackson who ran the Nettle Carrier Water Mill and kept the post office in his dwelling. Winnie married Bud Ci McDonald and now lives in Ivyton. She is a cousin of Sallie Jackson. Belle Smith daughter of Miller Bill Smith who worked at the Allred Mill on Nettle carrier creek below the Will McDonald place.

Emma Roberts daughter of George was an own cousin of Gov. Roberts and an exceptionally fine young woman. She is now 85 and lives in Cookeville. Her husband Doc McGee used to run a country newspaper in Livingston. Let me take time to mention Emma's sister Belle Roberts and her brother Frank of Taylor Cross Roads. Belle married a Mr. Edwards went west and died at the age of 76.

One day I was talking about Belle Roberts with Mrs. Delia Mullins and she agreed with me in what I'm going to say now, Belle Roberts was the prettiest woman that ever lived in Overton county regardless of my wife yours or any others.

Ella White whose father was Presbyterian minister was a sister of Jim and E. D. White married James Reed and is still living.

Mrs. Bud Q. Smith came to school with her husband. They kept house in a little building on the other side of Nettle-carrier creek about where Minor Smith's barn now stands. They crossed the swinging bridge back and forth to school. I think she was a daughter of Preacher Sewell who followed the hard-shell doctrine.

McDonald sisters daughters of Mike who when he was a school boy going to Greenhill school fell from the foot-log into the Nettle carrier in flood time and was pulled out again at the water fence clear down at the swinging bridge. When they finally revived him he was able to tell exactly what it feels like to drown.

Randy McDonald married Jim Linder. Kelly McDonald married Dick Sells their daughter was my last wife.

Here is a list of the boys I went to school with in this Lee school. Emit Winton son of Mitchell well-known citizen of Alpine for many years.

Leslie Winton brother of Emit I remember one day Leslie poured out 100 silver dollars on the desk in time of books after selling a fine colt. He was a clever fellow and could get away with anything in school. He is buried by Foster Winton near my old home.

Bud Q. Smith whose wife is mentioned earlier was a good math scholar.

J. B. McDonald brother of Belle and Viola mentioned earlier and of Mrs. Stephens by her first husband married a sister to Gov. Roberts. Their daughter Deane is Mrs. Ridley Mullins.

Burr Speck son of Harve Speck a big farmer in the Copeland Cove married a sister of Ridley and Walter Mitchell she's still living Ridley was attorney general of Tennessee.

George McGoglin came from Dry Hollow above Three Forks.

Fletcher White a brother of Jim and E. D. Will Smith brother of John married Etta Winton died at the farm back of Oak Dale school now known as the Liza Ferrell place, John Smith the oldest of Jim Smith's children.

John Choate from Fentress County he and I boarded together.

Thomas Jackson brother of Winnie McDonald now is Judge Tom Jackson of Texas.

J. M. "Tyce" Sells is the oldest man in this hollow known as a great chimney builder taught schools in many parts of this section.

Fate Keisling son of Charlie was my seat-mate later on in the George Gilbert school.

Fred Bilbrey was a good friend of mine.

About the time the Lee school was coming to a close I got a card from up in the Three Forks section urging us to ask Prof. Lee to come up there and teach a free school as soon as he got through with the one in Alpine. He agreed to do this so I went along and stayed at my father's place and attended that school too.

The next school taught in Alpine was the George Gilbert school. This was a subscription school it was begun in the fall of 1886. Prof. Gilbert left in the spring 1887 and one of his students Lansdon B. Robbins a fine scholar finished the school.

Among those who attended this school were. Girls Viola McDonald, Mollie and Ova Allison, Dada and Tiny Ledbetter, Florence and Etta Winton, Eva Copeland, daughter of John sister to Maywood married John Robbins brother of Lansdon, Fannie Ledbetter form Kentucky, Winnie Jackson, Belle Keisling Sonora Wood and sister to Mrs. Stephens, Nora Keisling daughter of Charlie, a big merchant head of school board for subscription schools she is a cousin to Belle Keisling Smith Mrs. John Smith she married Wash Hicks merchant of Monroe. Several small girls whose names I don't remember. Boys L. B. Robbins student under Gilbert finished the school for him. John Robbins son of Jim Robbins on Obey River, they boarded with Johnnie Robbins the Will Walker to Benton Norrod stretch of land was his farm, Marion Roberts son of George cousin to Governor and brother to Frank, T. A. Norrod cousin of Grant took typhoid and left school son of Benjamin R. still living but sick father of Cecil Norrod Alpine, Thomas Jackson, Tom Worley son of Old Baker Worley and lived near McDonald Chapel, Jessie Hancock was a fine fellow and a fine scholar he died in the west. Maywood Copeland son of John now lives below Livingston brother to John Robbins wife Eva who lives in the west, Pharis Wright Fentress County, George Winningham got killed as Sheriff of Pickett County trying to arrest a man son of John my first wife's own uncle, Hilary Vaughn son of Alvin brother of John a banker married Joe D. Hatcher's daughter, Emit Winton, John Smith, Willie Stuart, son of J.K.P. Stuart went to Texas and died an accidental death from a loaded shotgun, Geo. Hinds married Oss Winningham's daughter and lived in Livingston his wife is still living somewhere. J. L. Allison, Fate Ledbetter, Berry B. Ledbetter, Tice Sells, Fate Keisling, Willie Keisling half brother to Fate. These names call up precious memories and bring to mind faces that have changed with the years but when I see then in memory they are the same boys and girls I went to school with about sixty five years ago. Those were great days and sir I believe they have laid the foundation for a great future for our land. Sincerely Yours, A. G. Norrod Sr.

Inside view of a old school room at Alpine 1938

Notice how the desk are made with bench seat and tilt desk in front of the next one and one in the background old wood stove pipe and stove

Students playing ball out in field about 1938 at Alpine

Has written in center of roof in photograph
Rickman and Bilbrey

Location is unknown of this early mill located in Overton County or anyone person in picture. If anyone can identify this please contact the author this is real great old mill photograph.

SECTION III
Military

These are in the possession of myself at present. They were brought back to Overton County by a descendant of the original author of the letters. These were found in a old trunk in the attic in Indiana. Also is a picture believed to be the author along with this story.

Camp Cumberland Ford May the 8th 1862
Dear Wife I now take of the opportunity of writing to you to let you know that I am well an I hope that these few lines you well too I would lik to see you all I will come home as soon as I can you be the best you can.
I am yours W W. Cope A few lines from H A Clark I am well an doing well an I hope that these few lines well find you all well an doing well I send $22 in money to you an the children I want you to give the boys $2 and keep the other I send a note of $2.45 on John Boles an my Pocket Book to by James Pagett
So no more at Present
H. A. Clark

Camp near Stanford KY April 14 1863
Dear Friend after my respects to you it leaves me well I hope your health is improving I have to to my Regt again I can inform you that I saw your wife as I came out her and familywer well Reuben Clark is sstill under the Doctor the Rebels take him to Livingston and it tuck him two day to come back and he is staing at te house ande he is

Captain Calvin E. Myers

Camp Myers was named for the above he raised the company in Overton County for the Civil War, he was quoted as saying from an old newspaper article 1937 that they left for Celina on May 11, 1861 and then down the river to Nashville. His company was called the Overton Guards. He was elected Captain and had 107 men in his company at the time of the article in 1937 they were all dead except for him and Mike Speck Sr. He was also quoted in the article as saying he took part in twelve main battles of the war Cheat Mountain, W. VA., Port Royal, S.C., Corinth Miss., Murfreesboro TN, Chickamauga and Missionary Ridge Tenn, Rocky Face Ridge, Dalton GA., Resaca, GA, New Hope Church, GA., Dead Angle GA, where they got so close on us they would shoot your nose off; Kennesaw mountain where Gen. Polk was killed, then the defense of Atlanta for weeks; then Jonesboro; Franklin and Nashville. He said they said they surrendered under Gen. Joseph E. Johnson in North Carolina.

There could be so much more written this is just a short caption at this time.

Livingston Enterprise
April 1925

CAPTAIN J. K. DAVIS

By Alfred Lafayette Dale

Capt. Davis died March 15, 1925, He was a confederate veteran of the war of 1861 volunteer of Capt. T. S. Mackheny's Company of the 8th Tenn. Infantry commander of Col. Fulton's regimental of Calvary.

Capt. Davis at the time of his death was 84 years an 15 months old, living on his farm near Celina that his grandfather, William Dale settled on in 1799 or 80. His father was Mathew Davis, his mother, Elizabeth Dale, daughter of William Dale. He was a soldier under Gen. Jackson as was his father, Capt. Davis had four brothers, all Confederate soldiers three of them in Gen. Price army of Missouri. His five sisters, who are all dead, had Confederate soldiers for their husbands. One of them, Stanford Rich, of Braggs Army was killed at Murfressboro, in 1862.

Capt. Davis was very influential and had much to do with the elections in this county and was Clerk and Master for 12 years. He was an active supporter of the Democratic party, never voting for a Republican. Was never a candidate for office. He was a friend to all needy within his reach, was a large lumber and log dealer on the Cumberland for many years. He was an expert marksman with the old muzzle loading rifle; and enjoyed fishing immensely, as he was best fisherman in the county.

Col. Sam Davis Soldier

**The Livingston Post
Official Organ of Overton County**

Livingston, Tennessee, Thursday October 17, 1889

Circular Letter

The following named parties are respectfully requested to meet at the Court house in Livingston on Saturday 26th day of Oct., next for the purpose of taking the necessary steps looking to the organization of a "Confederate Home" and by so doing attach ourselves to the Association of Confederate veterans throughout the State and in the South generally, come one come all.

To wit: F. G. Bilbrey, C.E. Myers, A. L. Windle, W. F. Roberts, R. L. Burks, R. L. Mitchell, L. W. Chapin, A. J. Tompkins, A. W. Richardson, J. N. Cannon, John Cook, W. H. Parrigin, T. J. Webb, John F. Hancock, L. H. Hammock, A. P. Kimes, John H. Lea, William Allred, J. H. Copeland, F. M. Carr, Moses Miller, C.C. Carr, John M. Lea, Wesley Elam, J. W. Carmack, Pleas Buck, F. C. Allred, Jeff Bilbrey, H. L. Swift, J. H. Ray, Wm. Linn, G. K. Grimsley, F. H. Wisner, L.H. Nelson, Henry Jackson, M.V. Bilbrey, Thomas Reeder, Shelby Morgan, William Hunter, A. J. Sells, Elbert Hensley, Jesse Sewell, F. H. Daugherty, Sam Davis, John White, Pleas Huffeee, and C. W. Hill.

You and each of you are urgently requested to meet on the day above named at the house at 12 M. Oct. 8th 1889

C. E. Myers, L. W. Chapin, A.L. Windle, R. L. Mitchell, L. H. Nelson, J. N. Cannon, John Cook.

Henry A. Clark

Co. D 2ⁿᵈ TN Infantry

Henry A. Clark was born February 1, 1825 in Fentress Co. TN died August 12, 1909 in Pickett Co. TN married September 18, 1851 to Nancy J. McClellan born February 15, 1834 in Fentress Co. TN died May 10, 1910 in Pickett Co. TN she was the daughter of Fleming McClellan and Phoebe (Boles) McClellan. Henry and Nancy are both buried in the Polk Garrett Cemetery in Pickett Co. TN

James Madison Dulworth
8th Tennessee Inf.

James Madison Dulworth was born about 1841 in Cumberland
Co. Ky. He died about 1911, probably in Clay Co. TN (Then Overton
County). He married Mary "Polly" Cleary. Mary applied for a
military widow's pension. I have a copy of it.

Jasper Pleasant Zachary

CO. C 1ST KY CAV. U.S.

Jasper Pleasant Zachary was born February 22, 1841 in Fentress Co. TN died January 24, 1929 in Overton Co. TN he is buried in the Fellowship Cemetery in Overton Co. TN, he married June 13, 1869 in Overton Co. TN to Margaret E. Tranbarger born May 14, 1844 in Overton Co. TN died August 11, 1927 in Overton Co. TN she is buried in the David Sells Cemetery in Overton Co. TN.

Jesse Washington Carmack

Company D 8th TN Regiment

Jesse enlisted in 1861 in the Confederacy with Capt. Calvin E. Myers and served 4 years of the war. Jesse Washington Carmack was born September 1, 1841 in Overton Co. TN died June 9, 1924 in Overton Co. TN he is buried in the Mt. Gilead Cemetery in Overton Co. TN.

March 1916

OLD SOLDIER DEAD

Jesse Moore of the 2nd district of Overton County died Feb. 19th 1916, He was 86 years of age, and leaves a wife and four children, one son and three daughters. He and his wife had been married 65 years and his was the first death that had occurred in the family.

"Uncle" Jess Moore as everybody called him, was one among the best citizens of the county, had a large acquaintance, and was an old Confederate soldier; a strong Democrat; with many friends who will miss him. In his death the county has lost a substantial citizen; the wife a devoted husband; the son and daughters a good father.

Written by an old comrade in arm, who served with him in Gen. Dibrell's command

A. L. Dale

John Franklin Poston and Artelia with daughter Sally

Co. B 25th TN Inf. and later Co. A 8th TN Cav.

John Franklin "Frank" Poston born January 30, 1839 in Overton Co. TN died June 7, 1914 in Overton Co. TN buried at Falling Springs Cemetery. He married 2nd time to Artelia Allred in the photo above with daughter Sally, Artelia was born about 1843 in Overton Co. TN died February 18, 1915 she is buried at the Allred Cemetery.

John applied for a soldier's military pension and after his death Artelia applied for a widow's pension. I have copies of both of these

Joseph Michael Nation

I have a copy of his pension for service in the war between states. He was union army then. Pension has really good information.

Lard Hammock soldier

I have a copy of his pension application for service in the war between the states. He was in Confederacy.

Pleasant H. Wilborn

Co. B 8th TN Inf. C. S. A.

Pleasant H. Wilborn born December 15, 1841 died January 11, 1892 he was married to Sarah Ophelia Williams she was died July 21, 1908 they both are buried in the St. John Cemetery in Clay Co. TN. Although is what used to be Overton County.

Raleigh J. Thompson

Raleigh joined the Confederate Army in late 1862 as a member of the O. P. Hamilton's Tennessee Command, sometimes called Hamilton's or Shaw's Battalion. In February 1863, Hamilton's Command rode to Florence, Alabama and joined with General Forrest's Brigade. Many of Hamilton's Command were attached to the 8th Dibrell's Cav. Co. E. He served until the surrender and returned to Overton Co. TN and became a prominent country doctor in the 1st & 2nd Districts of Overton County.

Raleigh J. Thompson was born April 16, 1832 in Hamblen Co. TN died February 6, 1903 in Overton Co. TN and buried in the Dodson Chapel Cemetery in Overton Co. TN.

I have a copy of his pension application

William H. Bilbrey

Co. F 8ᵗʰ TN Cav. General Forests Brigade

William H. Bilbrey was born April 8, 1841 in Overton Co. TN died February 21, 1927 in Overton Co. TN he is buried in the Bethsaida Cemetery in Overton Co. TN.

I have a copy of his pension application for service in war.

William J. Allred Confederate Veteran Soldier

William J. Allred born July 15, 1842 Overton County TN and died May 20, 1915 Overton County TN he married Eliza Jane Nelson she was born June 23, 1842 in Georgia died March 26, 1921 in Overton County TN, they both are buried in the Shiloh Cemetery located in the Allred Community of Overton County. Have a copy of William's civil war pension application. Eliza's grandfather was Thomas Nelson from South Carolina who served in the Revolutionary War. I have a copy of his pension application.

Sam Cullom

COLORED SOLDIER DREW CONFEDERATE VETERAN PENSION FOR SERVICE IN CIVIL WAR

This is written on the application cover page it states Notice Applicants. The Negroes pension law passed by the Tennessee Legislature, provides that the Negroes pensioned by this Act must have actual bona fide residents of this State three years if they served with a Tennessee command, and ten years if they served with a command from any other State. They must have remained with the army until the close of the war, unless legally relieved from service. They must be indigent. Unless you come clearly under the law, it is useless to file a application. The board meets the second Tuesdays in January, April, July and October.

Sam Cullom was in Co. F 8th Tenn Inf. he filed his application July 9, 1921 and it was accepted. His application states I Sam Cullom a native of the State of Maryland and now a citizen of Tennessee, resident at Livingston , Tenn R.#3 in the County of Overton said State of Tennessee, and who was a servant from the State of Tennessee in the war between the United States and the Confederate States, do hereby apply for aid under the Act of the General Assembly of Tennessee of 1921. And I do solemnly swear that I was with 8th Tenn Inf Co. F in the service of the Confederate States, and that by reason of indigence I am now entitled to receive the benefits of this Act. I further swear that I do not hold any National, State or County office, nor do I receive aid or pension from any other State, or from the United States. I do further solemnly swear that the answers given to the following questions are true:

In what County, State and year were you born?

Answer: State of Maryland county not known and do not know date. I think I am 80 years or more.

Where did you [cannot read these two words they are blotched out]?

Give the names of the regimental and company officers under whom you master served. C. E. Myers, Captain Fulton's Regiment.

Answer: 1861 first Co. that left Livingston.

Give the name of your owner:

Answer: Alvin Cullom

What estate have you in your own right, real and personal, and what is its actual cash value?

Answer: No real estate, or personal property, live with my son who supports me.

What estate has your wife in her own right, real and personal, and what is its actual cash value?

Answer: nothing of any value.

State the gross income of yourself and your wife from all sources for the past year. This must include all money received either from wages, rents or interest on loaned money, if any. Also family supplies raised or received from rents and used by your family?

Answer: nothing.

How long and since when have you been an actual resident of the State of Tennessee?

Answer: Since I was 9 years old.

Have you an attorney to look after this application?

Answer: Yes

If so, give his name and address.

Answer: C. J. Cullom Livingston Tennessee

Witness my hand this 25 day of June 1921 Sam his X mark Cullom

Witnesses Geo O. Lea Witness Street and No. if any Postoffice Address Livingston Tenn P. O. Livingston Tenn J. H. Lea Witness R.F. D. (if any) #3 Postoffice Address Livingston Tenn

State of Tennessee Overton County I C. A. Verble Trustee of said County certify that Sam Cullom and his wife blank ____________ are assessed with none acres, valued at $___ and with $none of personal property. Witness my hand this 7 day of July 1921 C. A. Verble Trustee

If applicant and his wife have no property, the Trustee must so certify.

State of Tennessee Overton County

Personally appeared before my G. O. Lea of said County, the above named Sam Cullom the applicant, with whom I am personally acquainted, and having the applicant read and fully explained to him, as well as the statement and answers therein made, made oath that said statements and answers are true. Witness my hand and seal of office, this 25 day of June 1921. G. O. Lea.

State of Tennessee Overton County Personally appeared before me G. O. Lea a notary public of sad County, the above named Captain C. E. Myers and Mrs. J.H. Lea, two of the subscribing witnesses to the foregoing application, with whom I am personally acquainted, and known to me to be citizens of veracity and standing in this community, and who make oath that they are personally acquainted with the foregoing applicant, and that the facts set forth and statements made in this application are correct and true, to the best of their knowledge and belief, and that they have no interest in this claim and that said applicant's are good and free from dishonor. And Captain C. E. Myers further made oath to the following facts touching the applicant's service in the Confederate army. That his statements are true except he was in Co. D. at the beginning and later in Co. F. He further states that he was a very polite boy and performed faithful service and he further states that it is his best information that he served thru out the entire was and was with his

Co. when they surrendered C. E. Myers Witness my hand and seal of office this 25 June, 1921. G. O. Lea NP

Mrs. J. H. Lea further made oath touching applicants service in the army that she was a granddaughter of Alvin Cullom, and that Sam Cullom Col was sent away to the army with her uncle Jim and Ras Cullom at the beginning of the was and that he returned at the close of the war and told about how he buried Jim Cullom when he was killed in Atlanta and that it is her information that he served faithful thruout the war. Mrs. J. H. Lea Subscribed and sworn to before me, This June 25, 1921 G. O. Lea NP

Affidavit Letter attached to application:

George O. Lea
Lawyer
Livingston
Livingston Tennessee

July 8, 1921

Hon. John P. Hickman

Nashville Tennessee

Dear Sir:

Find inclosed application of Sam Cullom Col. for pension under col. man pension law acts 1921.

Sam Cullom Col. is a deserving negro and has no money and therefore cannot secure all the proof in his favor as several of the men who served with hil live a long ways from here.

However you will find a statement from the granddaughter of his master, and if this is not sufficient to satisfy the board please return the papers to me and I will secure such additional proof as you require as it can easily be had with a little expense.

I am a confederate soldier myself and have know this darky for a long time and I am assisting him in the matter because I know it is a deserving case.

Very truly yours, J. H. Lea Livingston Tennessee

** Please not that this was typed as it was read and the misspellings and words were not corrected they are just like they are his application copy that I have.**

Some additional family genealogy information on Sam Cullom to go along with this article he still has descendants living here in Livingston now his great granduaghter Alene Savage,she also has 3 other sisters living they are Ella Joyce Gist of Algood, TN, Juanita Page of Celina and Georgie Lee Hall of Franklin KY.

On the 1880 Census of Overton County in Dist.#6 Sam Cullom iis 43 years old born in Maryland, Permelia 40 TN , William 17 son TN, Etta 12 dau TN, Milla 9 dau TN, Jimmie 8 son TN, and Lou Fernia 1 dau TN. 1900 Census Overton County Tennessee 1910 Census Overton County Tennessee 65/4 1920 Census Overton County Tennessee District #6 Mack Cullom 61 m Hd TN md own farm, Ella

[Woods] Cullom 63 f wife, Fannie Maude 19 f dau. TN, Joe Claude 18 m son TN, Estella 14 f dau. TN, these first three children all moved to Detroit and died there. Lee Mint 11 f dau. TN she married Henry B. Gabbard from the Willow Grove area in Pickett County four of their daughters are listed above and are the descendants of Sam Cullom that we know of still living. Although they may be other descendants that we are unaware of.

Mack Cullom born August 15, 1858 in Overton County Tennessee died August 23, 1930 in Overton County and he is buried in the Bethlehem Cemetery in here in Overton County his wife Ella Woods Cullom born April 15, 1870. Mack was a Blacksmith by occupation and he owned a farm near where the present Overton County Fair grounds is today. Several other family members are buried in the Bethlehem Cemetery also besides Mack and Ella.Sam the father of Mack and the focus of this article he is the Civil War pensioner was born according to the census about 1835 in Maryland.

AN OLD SOLDIERS REMINISCENCES
Jake Shelton of Booz Has Colorful Career
As Soldier In Civil War
April 1931

J. J. Shelton commonly known as Jake Shelton was in Livingston on last Tuesday for the first time for years. His home is in the community of Booz Fifth District and is the same section where he was born 89 years ago. He is and has been for some time a bad cripple not able to walk without assistance. He enlisted in 1861 in the Confederate Army at Livingston in the organization of Capt. Joe Bilbrey's Company B 25th Infantry Reg. commanded by Lieut. Colonel Sidney S. Stanton, and while serving under Col. Sam Davis was discharged on account of disability at Tupelo, Miss., in 1862. After returning home some time after his discharge it became known to Capt. Tinker Dave Beaty who was commanding a company of Federal Guerillas operating principally in Fentress county and the Eastern portion of Overton county that he had arrived from the war and Capt. Beaty and his men sought his life and pursued him from place to place so that for his own protection he joined himself to a small bunch of confederate sympathizers commanded by Franklin Hammock and known as Hammock's men or Company. The two companies one led by Beaty composing of sixty to one hundred men and the other led by Hammock composing nine to fifteen men had frequent clashes and in the early part of the year 1865 they met and fought at a place known as Raven's Bluff on Puncheon Camp Creek in the Eastern part of Overton county when in battle Capt. Hammock and three of his men viz: William Hammock, James Ledbetter and Jack Copeland were killed. The remaining five men of Hammock's band made their escape by riding their horses over bluffs eight to ten feet high down the mountain according to reputable citizens. It is claimed that the signs of the horses shoes may be seen on the bluff of rocks until now.

This particular bluff and its surroundings were well known to Hammock and he had sought to decoy Beatty's men to this place for advantage but it happened that certain of Beaty's men were familiar with the bluff and it's surroundings and while a portion of Beaty's men were slowly following Hammock up the mountain certain of Beaty's men had gone around and gotten to the other entrance to the bluff which Hammock had planned to use as his exit in case of a retreat so that when Hammock entered that gateway to the bluff which was flat on top for a small space he found that he was trapped and when he found that he had been mortally still holding to his bridle he pulled himself up near his favorite horse an cut the horse's throat rather than let the animal fall into the hands of the enemy. On the morning of this battle according to reports Hammock and one of his most loyal men James Ledbetter made a pledge or vow to each other that in case one of them fell the other would remain with him and this James Ledbetter did Remembering his vow he remained after his chief had fallen and died with him. According to reports Beaty had at this time seventy nine men and Hammock had nine. The five of Hammock's men who escaped were George Gullet, John Brewington, Polk and Ben Speck brothers, and Jake Shelton the last named being the last survivor of the band known as Franklins men.

February 11, 1920 Article

In the spring of 1861 James McHenry made up and organized a cavalry Co. that was known as the Brown Rangers. I know of but four men living in Overton County who belonged to that Co. Bill Lynn, Tom Smith, Jim Garrett and myself. Bill Lynn was in prison at the time the second battle of Fort Donaldson was fought February 3rd 1863. If Tom Smith or Jim Garrett was not in that fight I suppose I am the only living man in Overton county that was. I would like to hear from these two men. Allison Cummins fell dying at my feet Robert Boyd and John Padgett were killed near me Jim Roberts standing at my side was wounded. The Brown Rangers were stationed at Livingston the old citizens remember them. The Company consisted of about 150 men it was first commanded by James McHenry later by Jim McMillin he was killed at Franklin James Amonett then became Capt.

B. F. Smith

CAMP ZOLLICOFFER
By A. V. Goodpasture
Article August 1936

The erection of the park and play ground with its thirty-seven acre lake, around the big spring at Zollicoffer is the realization of a beautiful dream that I have had toyed with for a long time. I believed it would make the most charming recreation spot in Tennessee. I have visioned the lake with its bold spring of living water at either extremity and I have thought though I might have been wrong in this that a hydraulic ram at the big spring might furnish water anywhere on the grounds and still leave enough waterfall to run a small dynamo that would generate electricity to light the entire premises. I know every foot of ground in and around the park. Before his death in 1896 it belonged to my father and I was reared there. He owned 1300 acres on both sides of the Gainesboro road and extending as far north as the top of the mountain. The big spring is in a small heavily wooded canyon which is round in form and covers three fourths of a circle north, east, and south, and slopes gently down on the west to the small valley, mostly on the west side of the branch, where Hiram Duke had a cabin some seventy five years ago and which is now to be covered by the Zollicoffer Lake. The Big Springs rises in the head of the canyon and gushes through a natural race of stone from its north and steepest side. After running a few rods it spreads out over a smooth shelf, almost straight across and falls in a beautiful cascade about six feet to the surface below. It then flows gently southwest and crosses the Gainesboro road where the dam will undoubtedly be built. My father built a brick house two miles west of Livingston on the east side of his farm where the Hon. T. W. Carlock now lives and moved out to it in 1860. I was then about five years old. The next year the Civil War cam on and the confederates established a training camp on my fathers farm called camp Zollifcoffer in honor of Felix K Zollicoffer who was soon afterwards killed at the battle of Mill Springs, Kentucky on January 19 1862. Between our house and the Big Spring was an open level field of some 25 or 30 acres which the soldiers used as a drill ground. The camp was on the west side of the drill ground near the spring and branch. There was a cabin on the south margin of the parade ground which was used as an armory. The commissary was south of the Gainesboro road in a building near the branch. Some of the officers I don't know how many boarded at our house and my brother Ridley and I regarded them as our friends. With the ownership of the ground and the friendship of the officers we felt ourselves entitled to the freedom of the camp. We went among the men and were petted and indulged by them. One of the officers whose kindness I shall always remember was Capt. James E. Rice,. He took us to the commissariat and opening a hogshead of brown sugar withdrew a sugar incrusted stalk of cane that had been placed there when the hogshead was packed. This to us was a great treat and a great favor. He undertook to teach us not very successfully now to make a wooden spoon without cutting our fingers and made us wise to other arts and crafts of the soldier. One day we concluded to inspect the armory and see what they had there, but when we reached the enclosure the guard halted us and ordered us to keep out, Ridley who was a little older and little bolder that I chose to assert his rights and continued on until the guard placing his bayonet against him forced him out. Bursting with rage and indignation he rushed to our friend Capt. Rice and told him how he had been bayoneted by the guard at the armory sympathizing with him Capt. Rice asked him if he would know the man if he saw him again. Ridley declared he would know him anywhere. Then Capt. Rice who had carefully unloaded his pistol handed it to Ridley and told him to go get his man. Ridley went directly to the armory pistol in hand. The guard dodged around the house Ridley discovered that his pistol would not shoot and the incident was closed except the guying the guard got from his buddies. While Capt. Rice was boarding at our house his wife came up from Dover to spend some time with him. I do not remember her visit but she and my mother became warm friends. I had no thought that I would ever see Capt. Rice after the war but when I went to Clarksville to practice law in 1877 I found him on the bench our Circuit Judge I was a stranger in Clarksville and was glad to find a friend there who knew my people. When I had an opportunity I called on his wife. She was cordial and friendly talking of my mother and my old home as she remembered them. Before I left she told me she had a very charming niece who lived some miles in the country and promised her to me as a sweetheart. Afterwards I met her niece and found her even more charming that she had been represented. And when she became my wife it was with the blessing of Aunt Jutes as her niece called her who had been in a measure responsible for bringing us together. Things happen that way and in this instance it had to do with Camp Zollicoffer and is therefore germane.

September 15 1917
COMPANIES M AND C GONE

It is said that a mother's heart is never immune to grief when forced to give up her child. For nearly eighteen months many have been the heart-aches caused by parents and friends having to part with the young men who have gone out at their country's call. When Company M left in May 1916 for the Mexican border there was hope that they would soon return which they did. But only to be called now to the trenches in Europe Company M left Nashville last Saturday for the training camp at Greenville SC and will doubtless be among the first to cross the Atlantic. All day last Sunday and for days a death like pall has hung over Livingston and surrounding country as the members of Company C paid their parting visits to loved ones. Many homes were like death chambers and religious services took on aspect of funerals. At 9:15 Monday the hour for the train to carry them away more than 2,000 people had gathered at the station. They came from far and near to bid the 100 young men Godspeed. Many carried memory boxes filled with those delicacies which only a loving hand can prepare. No brass band was here to thrill them with sweet music. No orator proclaimed aloud the inspiring words so common on such occasions. It was a quite determined procession showing at every breath and step the patriotism which prompted it to action. Strong men trembled and women wept as one by one our boys boarded the train. It was the grief of parting subdued by characteristic patriotism. The signal was given and they moved away in breathless silence save the waving of tear-stained handkerchiefs as the last act of encouragement. The trip to Algood was made as cheerful as possible by several ladies who accompanied the soldiers and at Algood the people proved their loyalty and patriotism by many tokens of love. And in behalf of the people of Livingston and Overton county and especially the relatives of these young men we want to assure the people of Algood of our lasting obligations for this token of sympathy and good cheer. Let us trust the wisdom of the All Seeing one that he may bring these boys back to us but should they fall in the trenches let us be consoled with the assurance that their live s were given in the cause of freedom to all mankind.

December 13 1916

A Note of Appreciation
Eagle Pass, Texas
December 2, 1916

This communication is address through the newspapers of Livingston to extend our thanks to the good people of Livingston for their many kindness to the members of Company "M" sicne the President's Call.

To the following named we are indebted for the best cakes we ever ate the box of cakes being received the day before Thanksgiving. Cake bakers Mrs. Eunice Keeton Miss Bettie Lou Keeton, Misses Nina and Ruth Farley, Miss Gertie Guthrie, Mrs. Dr. Zachary, Mrs. C. A. Roberts, Mrs. Cosby, Miss Geneva Bohanoon, Mrs. A. G. Keisling. Those who paid the express. Judge A. H. Roberts, Messrs. Stonecipher, C.J. Cullom, A. J. Mofield, Dr. Capps, Breeding, Mrs. Breeding, Mrs. Guthrie, Mrs. Keisling, Mrs. Laura Robins. Every member of the company had all the cake he could eat and if the donors could have seen the actual enjoyment expressed on the face of each soldier of Company "M" they would have been glad that they went to so much trouble. We also want to thank publicly all those who have previously sent cakes and candy to this company. This sort of thing is highly appreciated by the boys who feel that they are not forgotten. Life on the border is not __ sweet song but every man does and is expected ___ job. Al the boys are well and cheerful and are ready to come home as soon as they can be spared. Again thanking one and all I am.

Sincerely

J. W. Burks Captain

Co. M 1st Infty N. G. Tenn

December 3 1919
Soldiers Supplies

Dear Sir:

The Quartermaster's Department is so far undertaking to supply all of discharged soldiers sailors and marines for any of the following articles in all cases where the soldier at the time of discharge failed to receive the quota to which he was entitled when discharged.

1 oversea cap for all enlisted men who have had overseas service, 1 hat cord for all other enlisted men.

1 olive drab shirt

1 service coat and ornaments

1 pair breeches

1 pair shoes

1 pair leggings

1 barrack bag

3 scarlet chevrons

1 waist belt

1 set toilet articles (if lo possession when discharged)

1 slicker

1 overcoat

2 suits underwear

4 pair stockings

1 pair gloves

1 gas mask and helmet (if issued overseas)

If any discharged soldier, sailor or marine who did not secure all the above named when discharged cares to write to me stating the facts I will send him a blank to fill out to enable him to secure such property so long as the Quartermaster's department follows its present policy of thus supplying to each discharged soldier such of the above articles as he did not receive. Very truly Cordell Hull

Herman Copeland
World War II

Cordell A. Hammock born 6 May, 1921 died 12 Jan., 1945 killed
in action in France in WWII buried Liberty Cemetery

James "Jimmy" Hammock born 10 Apr 1828 died 12 Apr 1907
buried James Hammock cemetery he served in Co. D 25th TN
Inf. in C.S.A.

Thomas Gibbons standing at the tombstone marker at Maxwell Chapel Cemetery of his son Edd Gibbons born 4 Mch. 1896 died 21 Sep. 1918 he was a Private killed in action in WWI

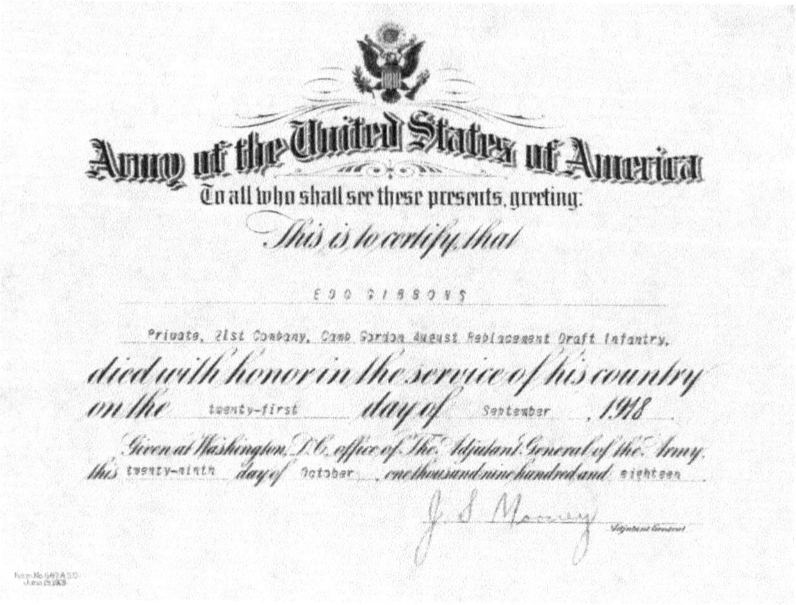
Army of the United States of America

To all who shall see these presents, greeting:

This is to certify that

EDD GIBBONS

Private, 21st Company, Camp Gordon August Replacement Draft Infantry,

died with honor in the service of his country on the twenty-first day of September, 1918.

Given at Washington, D.C. office of The Adjutant General of the Army, this twenty-ninth day of October, one thousand nine hundred and eighteen

Adjutant General

Document from the U.S. A. sent to the Gibbons family at the death of son Ed Gibbons for his service in World War I

COURAGE AND PATRIOTISM MARKED
OVERTON COUNTIANS IN WORLD WAR
County furnished more men according to population
Than any other in the United States many killed in action

Courage and patriotism is characteristic of the citizenship of Overton county as has been demonstrated by the number of soldiers furnished for service in every war in which the United States has been involved since the creation of the county in 1806 the spirit of Washington, Jackson, "Nolichucky Jack" John Sevier and the pioneers being a common heritage.Possessing a military spirit J. Willis Burks made up a company which was designated as Company "M" of the First Tennessee Infantry, in 1916 and was ordered to the Mexican border to protect the rights of the United States. Bohannon , first Lieutenant and Til J. Willis Burks was Captain, Shirley D. and H. Smith Second Lieutenant of this company. It was called away from the border in the spring of 1917 and in April 1917 transferred to the Second Tennessee Infantry for service in the World War. Captain Tim F. Stephens, Maurice M. Roberts and John A. Mitchell made up a company which was to become a part of the Second Tennessee Infantry Regiment and was called "C" company.

The company was headed by the following officers, Capt. Tim F. Stephens, 1st Lieut. Maurice M. Roberts, 2nd Lieut. John A. Mitchell, J. Willis Burks having been active and instrumental in making up this and other volunteer companies for the Second Tennessee Regiment, he was justly commissioned as Major in the regiment. The two companies left in September 1917, for training at Camp Sevier, S.C. where they remained in active training until May 1918. Soon after reaching Camp Sevier a re-organization of the Army was assembled was had and the Second Tennessee Regiment was annulled and the companies composing it were combined with older regiments. The commissioned officers retaining their commissions a portion of them along with the privates from Overton county and soldiers from other Tennessee counties and certain companies from North Carolina and South Carolina, principally composed the 119th Infantry and was affiliated with the 59th and 60th Brigades and was a part of the

30th Division which was justly called the "Fighting Thirtieth" and according to history no regiment in the Allied Armies find more effective fighting was exposed to more danger or bore more hardships than the 30th Division. It was this regiment of the 30th Division which was first to smash and go over the impregnable Hindenburg Line, which broke the morale and the courage of the German Army and virtually decided the war. Our own General Lawrence D. Tyson, of Knoxville the ranking military leader of Tennessee was one of the active commanders in the Thirtieth Division at the time the Hindenburg Line was broken. It was General later U.S. Senator Tyson who hurried to Europe to designate the correct location where the Hindenburg Line was broken so that a permanent marker could be set so that history might be correctly written and credit and honor be given to whom it was due having received information that another regiment was claiming that it had first broken the line and was about to succeed in having the marker set incorrectly to its credit.

Overton Countian's First

Among those first to go over this impregnable line of fortification were soldiers from Overton county. This county furnished two Volunteer Companies and the number of men furnished by Overton for the World War exceeded that of any county in the United States in proportion to the population, 600 men going to the Army and Navy from this county. The casualties from this county were forty. Many of them were killed in battle. Among the officers killed in action were Lieut. Shirley D. Bohannon, who frequently had charge of his company as Captain and Lieut. Tilman H. Smith, besides the casualties many of the soldiers from this county came home suffering from injuries received form poison gas, gunshot wounds, or loss of a leg or a arm. Many have been compelled to spend much time in hospitals and are diseased and maimed for life. A complete list of those enlisting from Overton county who made the supreme sacrifice follows. Lieut. Shirley D. Bohannon, killed in action, Private Walter E. Swack, drowned, wreck of the Ticonderoga. Corporal Lee. T. McCormack, killed in action.

First Tennessean Falls

Corporal Thomas G. Speck, killed in action first Tennessean boy to be killed in France. Privates Major McKinley, Oliver Ledbetter, Edward Gibbons, died of disease, Private Stone Frank Cherry Sims, killed in action. Lieut. Tilman M. Smith killed in action, Sergeant James Carson Guthrie, killed in action. Private Walter R. Hasting and Sergeant Wylie Sullivan, died of disease, Private Alonzo K. Smith and Bugler Shirley Lee Ledbetter, killed in action. Privates Willie B. Kendall and Hershel Clarence McBride died of disease. Private Robert Taylor Nevins died of disease on ship buried with high honors and prayer service at sea. Private James Waymon Hasting died of disease, Private Bynum Randolph, Sergeant Corbitt Richardson, Corporal Victor H. Koger, Private Dock T. Vaughn and Sergeant Wayne Scott Beaty, killed in action, Private Gordon Klope, Robert Norman Fletcher, Grover Cleveland Chandler, and Dillard Conner Sells died of disease, Sergeant Roger Quarles Lowe killed in action, Privates James Shirley Lee and Lee Copeland Hammock died of disease, Private Isham Buford Smith killed in action, Private Walter R Hensley and Joseph C. Cooper died of disease. Engineer Bailey Harrison Perry killed in action, Private Stephen Eli Langford, Hiram Smith and Willie E. Fletcher died of disease. The two named below not residence of Overton county but enlisted from Overton county.

Privates Willie R. Newman and Elisha Q. Garrett killed in action.

War 1812 Death
James Matthews has ties to Overton County

The massacre at Fort Mims occurred on 20th August 1813 250 whites butchered the children were seized by the legs, and killed by batting their heads against the stockading. Women were scalped and those who were pregnant were opened while they were alive. The creek Indians led by William Weatherford known as Chief Red Eagle the son of a Scot Trader. He preferred his mother's people Red Eagle was the leader of the Militant Red Sticks so called because they painted their war clubs a bright red color. The news of the massacre ran over Tennessee like wildfire. Governor Blount ordered Andrew Jackson to organize 2,500 volunteers and Miltia and John Cocke to do the same in the Eastern part of the state. "To Repel An Approaching Invasion". Jackson was recovering from wounds he received in a gun fight with Jesse and Thomas Benton at the City Hotel in Nashville, TN in early September all but one physician in Nashville recommended amputation of his arm. Jackson sent word to the volunteers that "The health of your General is restored" he said :He will command in person". On 7th October 1813 Jackson took command of his west Tennessee Army at Fayetteville in 1813 the state of Tennessee was not all settled and Overton county was in the west part of settled land in the state. Three days later they headed south to Huntsville, Alabama at the astounding speed of 36 miles a day (20 to 25 miles a day was good for militia). Hewing a road through the wilderness as they marched that provided a magnificent highway for future American settlers. They built Fort Deposit at the mouth of Thompson's Creek then moved on to the Cossa River and established a base at Fort Strother on 3rd Novemeber 1813 they encircled Tallushatee and systematically slaughtered most of the Warriors "We shot them like dogs". Reported Davy Crockett 5 men killed and 41 wounded they slew 186 braves (every man in the village). In this Battle Jackson found the Indian boy named Lyncoxa and orphan that Jackson raised as his own many hostile Indian villages wisely switched their allegiance to Jackson on of these was Talladega. When Red Eagle heard of Talladega change of allegiance he took a thousand braves to burn the village of about 154 people to the ground. Jackson set his men in motion 1,200 infantry and 800 cavalry on 9th November 1813 the army deployed for battle. 300 Indians lay dead on the battle ground the army losses 15 dead and 85 wounded. After burying his dead providing litters for the wounded Jackson swung his army back to Fort Strother.

James Matthews was wounded in the battle of Talladega that took place on 9th November 1813 he died on 11th November 1813 from wounds he received. James may have died at Fort Strother thirty miles north of Talladega. A muster roll record shows James deceased 18th November 1813. Research has turned up that James Matthews not only served with Andrew Jackson also with Davy Crockett.

Sources book used for above article were *Life of Andrew Jackson* 1977 by Robert V. Remini and *Life of Davy Crockett* 1854 by Albert J. Pickett.

The above article was written by a descendant of James Matthews who was Jim Loftis.

Joe Bob Poston soldier of WWI

His obituary from the Livingston Enterprise May 1956

He was the son of the late Richard and Elizabeth Crawford Poston, he moved to Cookeville about three years ago, he was a Veteran of World War I. Surviving are his wife Mrs. Auda Brown Poston, one daughter Miss Alice Poston of Cookeville, one son James Poston of Anderson IN, one brother Corbit Poston of Livingston, two sisters Mrs. Charles Conatser and Mrs. Marion Conatser of Livingston, one half brother Fed Poston of Rickman.

Local Marine Hits Bulls Eye
Article 27 October 1926

Proving his skill in the use of firearms while at target practice, John Harvey Lea, of Livingston, Tennessee recently requalified as a sharp shooter in the U.S. Marine Corps, according to an official target bulletin issued at Marine Corps headquarters her. John is 22 years old and was born near Livingston. He lived at the home of his father Alfred Lea, in Livingston before he joined the Marine Corps in October 1923. In recent weeks he has been stationed at Portsmouth N. H. Target practices are held by the Marine Corps at frequent intervals the men who qualify as expert riflemen are sharpshooters receiving medals and additional pay for their skill. Every man on the firing line strives to make high scores not only for a medal and extra pay but also for the keen sport of the shooting tests.

Soldier Writes From Korea
Article 29 August 1952

Mrs. W. L. Gillentine of Livingston recently received the following letter from her son William L. Gillentine Jr. who is in Korea

West Korea
10 August 1952

Dear Mom

I'm sitting here under a big chestnut tree the first one I've see in 20 years with a big chew in my mouth ritin and spitin. I have just been relieved and I'm waiting for a plane to fly me back in the land of the white Goks: This is the first day I've really had a chance to relax since

I've been here. I am still on the line but I'm so close to my bunker all I have to do is sneeze and I'll fall in it. My only worry now is that one these chestnut burrs will fall on my balding head. My relief is still talking about hot meals nice clean beds ice water and even television but he will get over that "dreaming" stage in a month or so. I am still on top of a hill overlooking Pannumjoini. We see the peace conference drive up and back nearly every day. The brass fly up in a helicopter. We can see the city without field glasses you can identify a man. The other day we were watching some activity near the conference meeting place. We saw a Chinese firing squad line up and they brought a young Chinese or Korean girl out and tied her to a post and shot her. We watch them shoot their soldiers now and then but this is the first girl I've seen them shoot. It almost caused an international incident here in the Marine division. One kid her from Kentucky said Ain't that a shame wasting women like that and scarce as they are over here. We have a lot of fun here in spite of the war. This is second war for most of the old timers in the company and when the kids complain we tell them about the big war. We even exaggerate a little like the boys form World War I used to do and still do. I believe I told you in one of my letters that they bury the dead (civilian dead) on top of the ground. Every cemetery has hundreds of mounds that look like small haystacks. The other day we found out why. They had a civilian funeral close by so we went down to watch. They set the corpse on the ground in a setting position and the women shoveled dirt up around him. (The women do all the work here). The men ran around the grave barefoot and stomped the dirt down. Every male member of the family brought a jug of rice wine and as they worked they drank and sang women and all. By the time they got the old goat covered up the whole shebang was roaring drunk and singing as loud as they could sing. I have never seen a happier bunch of people. This may sound kinda primitive to you but the Good Book says rejoice at death or words to that effect. Anyway they were really whooping it up I told the Captain if I got killed before I left here I wanted that same kind of funeral except I'd like for them to stretch me out for I can rest better in a horizontal position also to throw a cup of wine in my face now and then just to cool me off. He said since drinks were hard to get here he would send me back to Tennessee with the directions on how to bury me. I told him as strict as they were in Overton County about drinking they wouldn't have me half covered up till the whole shebang was locked up including me. This is a beautiful country kind like around

Livingston except there's not so much timber. The farms are mostly plantations and the land has been farmed for a thousand years before the birth of Christ and the land is still productive. I have never seen any modern farming machinery here they still plow with a wooden plow pulled by oxen. The wooden plow and the men lead the oxen the women do all the manual labor even work on the railroads, dig ditches etc. I think the men have really accomplished something there. I think I'll move over here after the war and buy a farm. I could teach Mitzi how to plow in no time at all. That would be a healthier occupation than pecking on a typewriter all day. Well the Chinka have started to drop a few shells around us so before they get the range. I think I'll crawl in my hole. These mortar shells give you and awful headache when they hit you. So for now I'll say so long to you and Korea. I'll see you in September.

Love Fate (William L. Gillentine)

Drafted Men Leave Saturday
19 September 1917

Below is a list of the boys of this county that were drafted. They leave her Saturday for Camp Gordon Shamblee, GA for their training.

Alfred Cooper, John B. Nivens, Minus Lee Cravens, Willie Herman Hawkins, Earnest Terry, Jas.W. Ramsey, Roy Howard, Lee T. McComack, Perry Hite Windle, Claud T. Keisling, Sammie Webb, Sherman E. Garrett, Willie Thomas Sewell, Alex J. Hammock, Farley White, Frank McDonald, Thomas A. Geisling, Ridley B. Matthews, James Beaty, Benson Seber, Uns Allen Cole, John W. Ford, Willie Dickerson, Elus Carter, Amos Winningham, Lee Copeland Hammcok, Less Kennedy.

Lee Copeland Hammock Soldier WWI

OVERTON BOYS LEFT TUESDAY
29 May 1918

The following Overton County men were inducted into military service on May 27 and entrained Tuesday morning for Camp Pike, Little Rock Arkansas. Before leaving the men were presented personal belonging bags and magazines by the local Red Cross. All of the men were in the best of spirits and carried the "Get the Kaiser" expression. A large crowd was the depot to see the boys off.

Chester B. Wilson, John T. Nelson, Harm Smith, Horace Warden, Willie T. Haycock, Booz Garrett, James Fred Creasy, James C. Swack, Sheridan Wilson, Elmer A. Langford, Granville H. Simcox, Thomas L. Oakley, Virgil Beaty, Herman D. Peak, Clovis H. Smith, Joe Bob Poston, Edd Eldridge, Aaron Ray, Oscar L. Poston, George B. Honeycutt, John H. Ringley, William Reubin Reecer, Isaac T. Sewell, Willie Matthews, Elmer W. Brown, Charles H. Vanmeter, Milton B. Daniel, Mike A. Phillips, Eddie Webb, Ezra Bilbrey, Charles D. Hill, John B. McCulley, Archie W. Green, Hassel A. Oakley, Fred Bowman,

John Copeland Setser, John L. Reeser, Stonman Newberry, Ernest H. Brooks, David G. Holman, Isaac B. Lynder, Tracy B. McCormac, William T. Masters, Herzhel Crabtree, Ernest A. Ashburn, Burrell C. Glasscock, George F. Rose, William Kinley West, Hester B. Bilbrey, Robert L. Ferrell.

Willie Matthews WWI Soldier

Elmer Langford WWI

Joe Bob Poston WWI

Ed Hammock WWI

John Edgar "Ed" Hammock born 7 February 1901 died 29 January 1980 he was son of Mack Benjamin and Martha (Poston) Hammock he is buried at Memorial Gardens Cemetery in Overton County.

Eddie Richardson WWI

Eddie born 17 March 1892 died 9 September 1972 buried at Richardson Cemetery in Overton County he was son of Peter and Melvina (Sells) Richardson

Final Thoughts from the Author

As with most history books, there just aren't enough pages within this work to accurately cover all the wonderful information we historians and genealogists want to share. I hope that this book leads to volumes of others—all equally enjoyed by those who prompted me to create this one. I'd like to thank all of the people who have had such kind words of encouragement about this project. I want this information recorded for our future generations…and I thank everyone involved in helping me through the whole process. My goal is to always use the 3P system. Preserve the Past. Protect the Current. Promote History. Thank you, friends. This book is for you.

Sincerely,

Ronald